THE PICK-UP

The PICK-UP

MIRANDA KENNEALLY

sourcebooks
fire

Published by Sourcebooks Fire, an imprint of Sourcebooks
P.O. Box 4410, Naperville, Illinois 60567-4410
(630) 961-3900
sourcebooks.com

Library of Congress Cataloging-in-Publication Data

Names: Kenneally, Miranda, author.
Title: The pick-up / Miranda Kenneally.
Description: Naperville, Illinois : Sourcebooks Fire, [2021] | Audience:
   Ages 14. | Audience: Grades 10-12.
Identifiers: LCCN 2021014766 (print) | LCCN 2021014767 (ebook)
Subjects: LCSH: Dating (Social customs)--Juvenile fiction. | Man-woman
   relationships--Juvenile fiction. | Mothers and daughters--Juvenile
   fiction. | Dysfunctional families--Juvenile fiction. | Romance fiction.
   | Young adult fiction. | Chicago (Ill.)--Juvenile fiction. | CYAC:
   Dating (Social customs)--Fiction. | Love--Fiction. | Mothers and
   daughters--Fiction. | Family problems--Fiction. | Chicago
   (Ill.)--Fiction. | LCGFT: Romance fiction.
Classification: LCC PZ7.K376 Pi 2021 (print) | LCC PZ7.K376 (ebook) | DDC
   813.6 [Fic]--dc23
LC record available at https://lccn.loc.gov/2021014766
LC ebook record available at https://lccn.loc.gov/2021014767

Printed and bound in Canada.
MBP 10 9 8 7 6 5 4 3 2 1

For a fan (and friend!)
who's been there from the beginning:
Andrea Soule

Content Warning

This book contains depictions
of abusive parenting.

FRIDAY

Mari

A black sedan pulls up in front of the curb.

The car has a dented rear end, and the passenger-side mirror is barely hanging on. It looks like it's taken a thousand road trips.

"Is this guy going to murder us?" I ask my stepsister, Sierra.

She chews her gum. "Does the license plate match what's on the app?"

I check the license plate against the one displayed on my phone. "Yeah. But listen. If we die, just remember it was your idea to do Ryde pool."

I open the back door and we slide inside. My seat cushion is held together with duct tape. How is this even legal?

The driver turns the music down. "Are you Mari?"

I nod at him in the rearview mirror, then check his name on my Ryde app. "And you're Charles?"

"That's right."

Once we've confirmed identities, the car edges out into

busy Friday-night traffic toward downtown. My dad's place is on Chicago's Gold Coast. Ever since he divorced Mom and moved away two years ago, I've only visited him a couple times. I'd never admit this to my mother, but I love this city. I can't get enough of it.

While Sierra scrolls on her phone, I take the opportunity to gaze out the window at Lake Michigan, so vast and blue it's practically the ocean. Boats full of sunbathers dot the surface. It's only six o'clock in late July, so the summer sun is still blazing.

It's a perfect night for a music festival—that's why I'm in town for the weekend. My absolute favorite artist, Millie Jade, is playing at Lollapalooza on Sunday. Listening to her music has gotten me through the best of times and worst of times, and I can't wait to see her perform live.

Sierra bought me a ticket as a gift for my birthday. As much as I worried about leaving Mom behind at home alone this weekend, Sierra's always been kind to me, and I couldn't turn down the opportunity to spend an entire weekend dancing at a concert.

The car begins to slow and turns down a side street. The driver turns the radio down. "Picking up passengers," Charles says.

Sierra insisted on the pool option so we could save three whole dollars, so other riders will be joining us. I'm praying they're not sketchy old men. How can I have the best weekend of my life if I'm dead?

The car rolls up in front of two guys.

Two very cute guys.

I glance at Sierra. She raises her eyebrows at them.

She scoots over to the door, forcing me to take the middle of the back seat.

"No, don't," I snap.

"You can thank me later," she replies with a smug smile on her face.

One of the guys climbs in beside me, and the other takes shotgun. The guy in front is definitely in college, or older, but the one next to me seems about my age. They must be at least six feet tall, and they're both buff like they play sports. To make a long story short—these boys do not fit in this tiny car.

By no choice of our own, the younger guy and I are sandwiched together in the back seat. Our thighs touch. Our arms touch. It's a game of Twister.

"It's kind of cramped in here," Mr. Buff says, adjusting his shoulders to get comfortable. "I might have to sit on your lap."

I lift an eyebrow. "Isn't the guy supposed to offer up his lap to the girl?"

He dramatically clutches his chest. "That's rather forward of you."

Sierra elbows me in the side and makes eyes at me.

A text from her appears on my phone screen: Dammmmmmmn he's hot.

He takes a sharp breath.

I flick my screen off.

Crap. Did he see what Sierra wrote?

I mean, she's not wrong. He has longish, messy, dark blond hair and his skin's tanned like a California surfer's. A smattering of dark freckles dots his nose, increasing his cuteness by a factor of gazillion. A leather cord with a silver charm hangs around his neck. A smartwatch and a collection of leather and cloth bracelets ring his wrists. His body definitely knows how to fill out that black T-shirt. Those muscular forearms look superhuman.

Even though it's hotter than the sun outside and we're nowhere near a forest, he's wearing a pair of hiking boots. What's that about?

"So this is Mari," my stepsister says. "And I'm Sierra."

I slap her thigh and shoot her a look. *What gives?*

I hear Mr. Buff take another sharp breath. He glances at me sideways, and nods with a small smile. His eyes are the same sparkling blue as the lake.

I don't think this guy is going to murder us.

We look at each other longer than strangers should. With eyes like those, it's hard not to.

"Since my very impolite brother isn't going to introduce us, I'm Tyler," the older guy in the front seat says.

"And who are you?" I ask the boy next to me.

"I'm T.J."

Well, hell-o, T.J.

T.J.

When it comes to girls, I have shit luck.

For most of high school, plenty of girls looked my way—to laugh at my jokes. To gossip with me. To ask for advice. To reach something on the top shelf.

A few even gave me sweet, shy smiles. Maybe they were interested in me?

But none of them ever full-on stared at me the way Mari is right now.

Her full lips part as she looks into my eyes. She has long, curly dark hair the color of a chestnut and wears rectangular glasses that look specifically hers, like how Wonder Woman's leather getup is made for her body. My eyes travel from her silver Converse high-tops up her long legs to a red leather skirt and white T-shirt.

Her clothes remind me of what girls wear to school dances. My worst memory flashes to mind, the time in middle school when I was slow dancing with Lacey Sutton, and it felt so warm and good that I leaned in to kiss her. As soon as our lips met, she ducked away. Wouldn't look at me. Never talked to me again. I guess she'd only agreed to dance with me as a charity case.

Even though girls had smiled at me in high school, I couldn't figure out how to talk to them, to take things up a level. What if the girl yanked away from me again? If that happened a second time, I'd apply to be an exchange student to Mars rather than face the shame.

My brother never had any problems getting a girlfriend.

To be honest, Tyler never had trouble doing much of anything.

4.0 GPA. Pick of colleges. Near-perfect math score on the SAT. Star of the high school tennis team. He secured a job at a hedge fund an entire year before he graduated from the University of Chicago.

When Tyler was home for Christmas break last year, I confided in him about my total lack of girl experience. While we were playing Xbox, when our eyes were firmly planted on the TV screen—so Tyler wouldn't see how embarrassed I was—I asked for help.

"How can I meet a girl? One who, like, wants me?"

"If you like a girl, just talk to her."

I scoffed. "Yeah, like that's ever worked. If I'm alone with a girl, nothing happens. We end up talking or goofing off. They aren't into me."

"If you're not making a move, they probably think you aren't into them."

Huh. I'd never considered that, but it made sense. In the fall, I'd gone with my parents to Dad's company picnic and ended up wandering around with Samantha Henley. She and I had such a good time together. Afterward we ditched our parents and went out for fro-yo. Honestly, it never occurred to me to kiss her. I'd always been so worried about rejection, I kept things casual.

After telling my brother about Samantha, he looked at me like I was from an alien planet. "Dude, if she spent all day with you, of course she was interested. You should've made a move! Next time you have to kiss the girl, okay?"

Easy for Tyler to say.

Besides, Sam couldn't have been that interested. A few weeks later she had a boyfriend. But what if I had found the courage to make a move?

"So what do I do?"

"You need to have more confidence," Tyler said, tapping his video game controller. "Then you'll be able to get whoever you want."

"Yeah right."

He held his arms out wide, the controller dangling from his hand. "I don't have any problem getting girls."

"Yeah, but you're you and I'm me."

"You look just like me, Teej."

I studied my older brother. We're both tall, and our faces are so similar we could be twins, but while my body looked like a strand of spaghetti, his arms were corded with muscles. He could bench-press me. He could probably bench-press a T. rex.

"I don't have your body, though," I said.

He set the controller on the carpet and stood. "Change your clothes. We're going to the gym."

Normally I'm careful about asking my brother for advice because he has definite views on what I should and shouldn't do. Sometimes I like his ideas, but others are way out of my comfort zone. But in this case, I loved it.

Thanks to strength training and drinking tons of protein, I've put on fifteen pounds of muscle this year. And this summer, when I wasn't at the gym, I've been working for a landscaping company. Hauling mulch makes you ripped. On top of that, being out in the sun has tanned my skin. For the first time ever, I'm proud of my body and love how strong it is. I pushed hard for it.

I look like my brother now.

But there are other complications. Like... I don't know how to make a move. I'm the world's last eighteen-year-old virgin. The absolute lastest of the last. If I were the only guy on Earth, humanity would go extinct because I'd never gather the courage to approach someone about repopulating the species.

When I asked Tyler how to ask a girl out, and maybe even about fooling around, he just shrugged. "Find somebody who sets your blood on fire. Then you'll know what to do."

And now I meet Mari, this gorgeous girl—maybe the most gorgeous girl I've ever seen. She has a deep Southern accent. When she says "Hi," it sounds like "Hai," and I'm a goner.

She smells like springtime.

My blood is on fire.

But I'm never going to see her again. This is what, a ten-minute car ride downtown?

See what I mean? I have shit luck.

Mari

Sierra elbows me again.

I elbow her back.

Yes, this guy is cute. Sexy, even. But he's way out of my league.

T.J. grasps the roof handle above the door, showing off his impressive biceps. With his other hand, he taps his knee with the tips of his fingers. He seems comfortable and at ease. What's that like?

He's a stranger, but I'm not worried. After Dad left, Mom signed us up for self-defense classes. They helped make me strong, and to be honest, kind of a badass. Mom was more excited to have a reason to let off some steam and punch things, especially the class dummy we all called Asshole Bob.

T.J. doesn't seem creepy, but even if he was, I could take him down like the time I totally incapacitated Asshole Bob with a few jabs to the sensitive shoulder area and a hard knee to the crotch.

"What does T.J. stand for?" I ask.

"Terrific and jazzy," T.J. says, making jazz hands.

"It stands for Thomas Jefferson," Tyler says with a snort. "Our dad's a history buff."

"And he clearly hates me," T.J. adds.

"T.J.'s not a bad name," I say.

"The name Thomas Jefferson is pretty geeky, though, and not the best guy to be named after." T.J. gives me a sneaky smirk. "Dad ruined my life. That's why I'm hanging out with my brother on a Friday night."

Over his shoulder, Tyler playfully flips T.J. off.

Sierra goes back to tapping on her phone. Tyler's head is bobbing along to the driver's rap music. The car zooms along Lake Shore Drive toward the skyscrapers in the distance.

I can see T.J. looking at me out of the corner of his eye.

That's when the truck in front of us suddenly brakes.

Our car screeches to a halt.

T.J. throws an arm out to protect me.

His hand grabs my boob.

My boob.

The momentum from braking jerks me to the side, straight into T.J. I reach out to grip anything to steady myself, and fall onto...little T.J.

"Ahhh!" he yells, covering his lap with his hands.

"Oh my God I'm so sorry," I blurt, trying to sit up.

The driver whips his head around to face us. "Man, did she hit you in the junk?"

"Ohhhhh nooooo," Tyler groans.

Sierra doubles over laughing.

"Don't sue me," the driver pleads.

"Do people sue when they get hit in the junk?" Sierra mumbles to me through her laughter. "What if T.J. sues you? We'll have to get a lawyer."

"Could you pull over?" I ask the driver. "This looks like a good place for me to go die now."

Tyler is howling laughing along with Sierra.

"Do you really want me to stop?" the driver asks.

"No, I was joking. We don't want to be late," I say.

As the car begins to move again, I clench my eyes shut. I hit a stranger in the nuts. Isn't that the worst thing that can happen to a guy? I'm pretty sure it is, based on my self-defense lessons.

"I'm so sorry," I say again.

"Hey, it's okay," T.J. says softly. "You didn't hurt me."

I open my eyes to look up at his. "Are you sure?"

"It was, um...a close call, but I'm fine." His face is rapidly turning a bright shade of red. He coughs into a fist. "Did I, um, hurt you? You know, your, um, chest?"

"Dude, you hit her in the boobs?" Tyler shakes his head, covering his eyes.

"Can you pull over?" T.J. asks the driver. "I'm going to go die now too."

That makes me laugh, and he joins in with me. I like his sense of humor.

He runs a hand through his blond hair, mussing it, then licks his full lips. Again, he peeks at me sideways. He seems like a nice guy. A sweet guy. The kind of guy my friend Rachel would refer to as boyfriend material.

Me?

I wouldn't know.

T.J.

Aside from nearly getting hit in the nuts, maybe my luck isn't
that shitty today.

It was pretty good luck my brother wanted to go eat at this
Mexican place he likes on the North Side. Otherwise, we never
would've caught a Ryde from there. We wouldn't be in the car
with Mari now.

But will my luck keep?

I hold my breath, expecting the driver to drop the girls off by
Ohio Street Beach, the section of Lake Michigan where people
like to cluster their boats in an armada party, so they can drink
and dance together.

But we drive on by.

Then we pass Navy Pier, where the Ferris wheel sparkles in
the early evening sunlight. Both off to the right and dead ahead,
skyscrapers loom over us.

Any minute now, this car is going to leave Mari someplace.

Maybe she's going on a date, or to her boyfriend's place? Maybe she's on her way to the hospital to visit a sick relative, and I'm the asshole creeping on her.

I roll my shoulders. What the hell's wrong with me? I don't want to be that weird guy in the Ryde.

But it really doesn't get weirder than grabbing a girl's boob, right?

I groan under my breath. I've just decided to put her out of my mind and move on with my life when Sierra speaks.

"What are you guys doing tonight?"

Tyler looks over his shoulder. "Going to Lollapalooza. Shit's gonna get crazy! Wooo!"

I cringe. I'm beginning to worry Tyler had one too many margaritas when he was pregaming at the Mexican restaurant. He never drinks in front of my parents, so I've never been around him while he's this buzzed before. What if he scares the girls?

"We're going to Lollapalooza too," Mari says, and my pounding heart threatens to rip out of my chest. "I'm in town to see Millie Jade."

"Oh." My voice sounds tiny and disappointed. "So you're not from Chicago?"

She shakes her head. "My dad lives here. I'm from Tennessee. I live there with my mom."

"Do you visit a lot?"

"Not as often as she should!" Sierra interjects, and the girls slap each other's legs and mumble "Stop it!" at each other, and I'm left wondering what that's all about.

"How about you?" Mari asks me. "Where do you live?"

"Madison, Wisconsin, but I'm going to school here in the fall at the University of Chicago." Her eyes light up at that. I gesture at my brother. "And Tyler lives here now. I'm staying with him for the weekend."

Tyler pumps his fist. "It's our bachelors' weekend, baby."

"Not that kind of bachelors' weekend," I add quickly. "I'm not getting married or anything."

Sierra pokes her head around Mari to smirk at me. "That's good news."

The two girls elbow each other again, and I have to fight not to grin.

Our car is getting closer to the music festival in Grant Park.

I glance down at my phone. According to the Ryde app, we're about two minutes from our drop-off. This is my last chance to make a move. If I don't say something now, this will be it. I'll never see her again.

My heart pounds in my chest. A buzzing sound fills my cars.

I give myself a pep talk: *What do you have to lose? If she turns you down, it's not like you'll be running into her in the lunch line at school while waiting for the mystery meat.*

"Do you, uh, want to walk around at the festival tonight?" I find myself asking.

Mari lifts her eyebrows. Then she looks at my eyes and tilts her head. "Like hanging out?"

"Yeah."

Considering me, she worries her bottom lip. "Okay, why not?"

I grin, and start to pump my fist in celebration but stop myself just in time. I don't want Mari to think I'm a total nerd. I play it cool.

My brother, however, goes, "Nice one, Teej!"

And that's when I die of embarrassment.

The car rolls to a stop near Grant Park. Music blares, and my pulse beats along with the roaring bass.

Tyler told me lots of different kinds of people come to Lollapalooza. Everybody from metalheads to pop fans. I'm into many kinds of music, especially EDM and metal, the kind that pulses with color. Based on the beats and the excitement outside the car, I can tell I'm going to love this.

I climb out, then reach back to help Mari up from the back seat. Our eyes meet as she stands, and she gives my hand a little squeeze before dropping it. With a quick glance at me, she adjusts her purse against her hip and pats it.

Once the car is gone, we move off the sidewalk and onto a patch of grass.

Tyler is already tapping on his phone. "Should we give that driver a bad rating? Leave a review saying he's responsible for my brother being unable to have children?"

Sierra and Mari crack up.

"Don't write that," I tell Tyler. "Give him five stars. I'm happy."

Mari's face blushes. "So my sister's meeting up with friends from school."

"Tyler is too."

I still can't believe Tyler invited me to hang out with him and his friends. This is the first time he's ever asked me to visit him in Chicago. I'd never say this out loud to him, or to anybody, but hanging out with him is a big deal. He's, like, my favorite person and everything I want to be.

We fall into a sea of people waiting to get into the security tent. Electric excitement buzzes around us, as the crowd talks about the festival. Up ahead is an archway, with *Lollapalooza* painted in bright bubble letters. I glance around to see similar artwork in the distance.

At some point I'll have to sneak away from Tyler to check them out. I've always enjoyed painting and drawing in art class, making any kind of art with my hands, but graffiti is a new interest of mine. Not that I can tell anyone.

People don't generally approve of vandalism. Unless you're Banksy, and then people are all, *Please sir, paint whatever the hell you want on my building.*

First time I thought about it, Dad was driving us home from visiting Grammy in Milwaukee a few months ago. We were driving under an overpass when the sun broke through some clouds. It made me think about aliens transporting down to earth.

And that started my obsession: I had to go paint a green alien under that overpass.

My fingers itched. Every time I closed my eyes, I dreamed of him.

I went to several construction supply stores. Craft stores too. Finally I found the right color of green and bought several cans. Snuck out in the middle of the night, drove to that overpass, and painted my little alien.

But that was the one and only time I've done it. I scratched the itch. *That's enough*, I tell myself.

What if I did it again and someone caught me? Got arrested? Would the University of Chicago rescind my acceptance and tell me to get lost? Probably.

But deep down? The itch is still there. Clawing up to the surface. Desperate to shake a bottle of spray paint, uncap it, and fill a blank piece of concrete with my dreams.

How do you get a gig painting boards at concerts like this? The moment the idea enters my mind, I shove it to the side.

Art isn't a real job.

People jostle us as they try to push closer to the front of the line. The hot air reeks of beer, body odor, and weed, but my mouth waters at the smell of pizza that somehow cuts through all the other gross scents.

I glance down at Mari. She's several inches shorter than me. It's cute how she adjusts her glasses, pushing them up on her nose.

"I don't know about you," I say. "But I am dying for some deep-dish."

Her nose wrinkles. "I'm more into New York style than Chicago."

"How can you not like deep-dish?" I exclaim. "All that gooey cheese? I live for it."

"It's just too heavy for me... Plus, I like being able to fold my pizza in half." Hearing that makes me smile. "Oh!" she adds. "I can't wait to get some Garrett's popcorn. Do you think they'll be selling it here?"

I give her a shrug. If they don't have it, I could easily invite her over to Michigan Avenue to find some, but I don't want to seem too forward. On the other hand, she did agree to walk around together tonight, so that must mean something, right?

Tyler reaches into his pocket and pulls out a multi-colored wristband for me that says *3-day pass*. He snaps it on my wrist.

His white wristband shows he's allowed to drink. I could use one right about now. I invited a girl I don't know to hang out with me. Now we're just standing here in line not saying anything, as our siblings play with their phones.

Speaking of siblings, it's hard to believe Mari and Sierra are related. Mari is short and slim with dark hair and fair coloring, while Sierra is a blond who looks strong enough to be a Viking, or at least captain of a rowing team. She's taller than me, and her biceps are cannons. If I challenged her to a push-up contest, I'm not sure I'd win.

"You and Sierra don't really look alike," I say.

"She's my stepsister. My dad remarried a couple years ago," she grumbles.

She sounds angry. I know how lucky I am that my parents are still together. Several of my friends' parents are divorced, and they feel caught in the middle.

"Is it just you and Tyler, or do you have other brothers and sisters?" she asks.

"Here's my little brother, Teddy." I tap my phone screen to show Mari a picture of our dog, a hound mix we adopted from a local shelter.

"Aww," she says. "He looks just like you."

"Dashingly handsome?"

Mari laughs. "I bet he's humble like you too."

I take a chance and nudge my shoulder against hers.

With a quick glance at my face, she swipes a lock of curly hair behind her ear, then checks her phone.

"What bands and singers are you excited for?" she asks.

"My favorite band If We Were Giants is here. That's why Tyler invited me."

"I haven't heard of them."

"They're, like, hardcore metal."

"That doesn't sound like my thing."

"Actually, I bet you'd like them a lot. They mix in some electronic club music and do covers of pop songs that are really good. They do one of Taylor Swift's even."

There's a long pause, and I'm wondering if she's picturing me differently now that she knows what kind of music I like.

I hate olives. They're the worst food ever. I'd rather eat island bugs like people on *Survivor*, but my mom says there is a variety of olive on earth for everyone. Even though I haven't found it yet, I keep trying olives to see if I find the one.

So I get that plenty of people don't like metal, but I'm convinced there's a metal song for everyone. Even Tyler, who mostly listens to rap and pop, likes If We Were Giants.

I played their song "Glad You Came" for him and he said, "This song slams."

Only Tyler could say something "slams" and make it sound cool. I was so happy he approved of my favorite band.

Still, metal might be too much for Mari.

"Millie Jade, huh?" I say. "Anybody else you're looking forward to?"

"Tonight I want to see Shawn Mendes."

I crinkle my nose like she did at the idea of deep-dish pizza. "Really?"

She gives me a little shove. "Yes, really! He may not be as pretty as you, but he has a nice voice."

"Me? Pretty?"

"Oh, please. Look at you. Are you photoshopped?"

Mari

Did I really just ask if he's photoshopped?

Am I sick? Should I take my temperature?

When it comes to boys, T.J. seems easy to talk to, and I guess that means I need to be careful when opening my mouth. Lord only knows what might come out next.

I need to change the subject. "Have you ever been to Lollapalooza before?"

T.J. shakes his head. "This is the first year my parents have let me come."

Sierra looks up from her phone. "Ours too!"

"My dad says wild things happen here," I add as the line edges forward. "He said one year a guy walked around naked only wearing a python."

"Oh, he heard about my outfit then?" T.J. jokes.

My face heats up at the idea of him without any clothes.

"You would not believe what happened to me last year," Tyler pipes up. "Me and my friends started drinking before noon, and I don't even remember most of Saturday afternoon. Apparently I drank a little too much and had to go to the med tent, and I slept right through Coldplay, which was the band I wanted to see most."

T.J. nods. "Don't get drunk and sleep through your favorite band. Check."

I laugh. "Noted."

Moving as fast as turtles, we edge closer and closer to the security tent. Once there, we step through metal detectors. A security guard thoroughly searches my tiny purse, which barely holds my bank card, phone, and lipstick, so I don't know why they think I could fit a weapon in here.

Next a festival worker scans my wristband.

Then we're finally inside!

Every summer, a music festival called Bonnaroo descends on my hometown of Manchester. It takes place on a huge piece of farmland only a few miles from my house. Bonnaroo's always been super crowded, but Lollapalooza feels even more so.

The crush of concertgoers fans out in all directions away from the entrance and toward the various stages.

The first thing I see is a massive Lolla Shop tent, *because capitalism*. The colorful T-shirts on display remind me of my best friend, Austin. No matter where he goes—even like middle-of-nowhere Arkansas—he always has to buy a souvenir tee. He must have hundreds at this point.

I snap a picture to text him.

Me: Which shirt should I get you?

Even though I know Austin's phone is tethered to his hand at all times, he doesn't answer immediately. I wait for my cell to beep, but it stays silent. My eyes begin to burn with tears.

Two minutes later, my heart soars when he finally writes back: Anything's fine. Pick whatever you want

I shut my eyes. Before everything changed, he wouldn't have hesitated to tell me exactly which shirt he wants. Now it's, like, we're still friends, but it's a lot harder to stay close to each other. A wall went up between us. I mean, I get why, but it sucks all the same.

In elementary school, girls went one way on the playground and boys went the other. Being friends with a boy wasn't something I'd ever considered.

Not until him.

I've been friends with him since middle school, when we were assigned to be lab partners in biology class. The first day, he said, "Thank God you're my partner."

I'd raised my eyebrows in response. He always made the honor roll in elementary school. It wasn't like he needed me to make a good grade.

"I mean, I'm glad I'm not stuck with a freeloader," he added, folding his hands behind his head and leaning back on his stool. "You're better than me at this stuff."

I grinned, happy that he wasn't threatened by me. I'd always had the top math and science scores in our grade and knew from experience that some boys hated when I out-schooled them. I'd been on the receiving end of dirty looks, and other kids called me a "know-it-all teacher's pet" more than once.

Every day before class started, Austin and I would sit at our lab table and talk about whatever. Mario Kart. What we ate for dinner the night before. How we both wanted to go to Florida for vacation. Him: baseball spring training. Me: Disney World.

Talking to Austin was easy. As we grew older, our conversations changed. We talked about what worried us. What scared us. Austin told me how his dad always rode him hard to *make better grades already* and *run faster to first base*. I even told Austin what was going on with my parents, how much it hurt when they decided to get divorced.

He always listened, always cared.

What I didn't know was that he liked me as more than a friend.

One night several months ago, toward the end of junior year, Austin came over to do homework. We were sitting on the living room floor, watching TV and working on calculus, when he suddenly leaned over and kissed my mouth.

At first, I paused frozen in shock, but then it felt warm, and cozy, so I leaned in and kissed him back. I wasn't thinking about anything except how nice his mouth felt. When I finally came to my senses and realized I was kissing my best friend, I pulled away and walked him to the front door.

"Let's talk tomorrow," he said with a gentle smile.

I passed him the black cowboy hat he wears everywhere, gave him a hug good-night, and totally panicked. I had no interest in dating him.

I couldn't fall asleep that night. Why would Austin kiss me? He was cute. He could be with whoever he wanted at school.

The kiss was nice, but it had to be a one-time thing. Dating leads to disagreements, which leads to fighting. Which leads to breakups.

I'd rather be alone than risk losing someone I care about. Especially someone I love as much as Austin.

The next morning at school, he was striding down the hallway toward me in that cowboy hat of his with a big smile on his face. He came right up to my locker and leaned in to kiss me. Totally something a couple would do. I pulled back.

Wrinkles formed on his forehead.

As a kid, the idea of quicksand terrified me. If I started to sink in it, how would I pull myself out? I couldn't do a single pull-up during gym class.

I worried about falling into quicksand on the playground. At the beach. Even random places like the park and outside the grocery store. Pretty much everywhere. I didn't understand you weren't likely to sink in quicksand in Manchester, Tennessee.

In that moment with Austin, I hoped the floor would turn into quicksand and swallow me whole.

With a deep breath, I told him, "You're my best friend, and I love you, but I don't want a relationship."

His face crumpled, then he pulled off his hat and leaned his forehead against mine. "We would be so good together."

Deep down I knew it could be true, but I wasn't willing to try us as a couple on for size. I wasn't doing that with him. Not with anybody.

"I'm sorry," I whispered to him, and with a red face, he turned and stormed off down the hallway. He didn't show up in calculus. Later I found out he skipped the rest of the day and went to Normandy Lake to be alone. I cried when I pictured him sitting on the tailgate of his truck, gazing out at the still water.

Now? Nothing is the same. Austin never hugs me anymore. It takes forever for him to text me back.

I look up from my phone at T.J. He's laughing at something his brother said and pointing off into the distance. T.J. slowly turns his head, and the wide smile he gave his brother becomes shy and sweet as he finds my eyes. Looking at me, he pulls a deep breath, his chest puffing out. I feel a sudden urge to rest my head against it and hug him.

I shove those emotional desires deep down inside me. I can't risk that.

I've already hurt Austin.

I don't want to hurt anybody else.

I huddle with Sierra, T.J., and Tyler as the crowd bustles around us.

"My friends are meeting at Tito's stage to see Foo Fighters," Tyler says in a raised voice so we can hear him over the roar of the crowd. "You guys want to come?"

Sierra shakes her head. "We're going to see Rosalía first. My friends are waiting for us there."

"I could go with you," I say to T.J. "I'd rather see Foo Fighters." Which is the truth. I've always liked that band.

Sierra takes my arm, pulling me a couple feet away from the boys. "You're supposed to stay with me, Mari."

"I will be with you...at the larger Lollapalooza festival."

She bites her lower lip. "Mom and David will be pissed."

"They won't know if we don't tell them."

"We're supposed to check in with them together."

"So let's do it now." I pull out my phone and open the Skype app.

Sierra's eyebrows furrow. "I got us these tickets so we could hang out, you know. Not so you could run off with some guy."

I'm the worst kind of friend and stepsister, putting a guy first. "You're right. I'll stay with you."

"Nah, just kidding, I'm messing with ya." Sierra pushes my shoulder and bursts out laughing. "I don't care. T.J. is seriously hot. You need to go get some of that."

Before Austin, I kissed a few boys when I was younger, at camp and at school dances. I enjoyed it. I wouldn't mind making out with a guy like T.J.

It's not like anything serious could develop between us. He's going to college in Chicago in the fall, while I have another year of high school in Tennessee. If it's only a weekend, it's not like I could hurt him.

Maybe it would be okay to have a weekend fling. A weekend fling and nothing more.

T.J.

"**What do you think they're talking about?**"

Tyler shrugs. "Probably making plans so that you can hang out with Mari."

I take a deep breath.

My brother pats my shoulder. "You okay?"

"Nervous, I guess. I like her. Do you think that's nuts? I mean, that I could like someone I just met?"

Tyler puts his hands in his shorts pockets. "I think it's normal to know when you're into somebody."

Mari glances over at me with a worried look on her face.

Tyler nods at her. "You should offer to go with them instead of hanging out with me. They're probably nervous about splitting up."

I rub my palms together. "You're right."

"Let's plan to meet up at the Perry's sign at eleven tonight. Text me if anything changes." Tyler pulls out his wallet, digs in it for a second, then pulls out a condom. Then he cocks his head, thinks for a second, and pulls out two more condoms. He passes me all three.

Shit. I shove his hand away. What if Mari saw that? "I'm not going to need those."

My brother smirks at me. "You never know, man. Just take 'em."

With a quick glance around, I grab them and push them deep into my pocket. "Don't you need them?"

He holds up his wallet and shakes it. "Plenty more where that came from."

"How do you fit them all? Is your wallet a clown car? Open it up, and more and more condoms keep pouring out?"

"Sure, let's go with that." Before he walks off, he turns around and points at me. "Make sure to either use those, or take them out of your pocket before Mom does the laundry. Trust me, you do not want to deal with that."

I cringe.

After patting my pocket to make sure the condoms won't fall out, I walk over to Mari, praying she didn't see what my brother gave me. I'd hate for her to get the wrong idea.

With a deep breath, I tell her, "I'm up for seeing whoever, as long as it's with you."

My words come out cheesier than I figured they would, but they surprise Mari and make her smile.

"I was telling the truth about seeing Foo Fighters," she says. "My dad always played their music when I was little."

"Let's go then," I say, taking her hand. It feels warm and just right.

She looks down at our hands linked together, and inhales sharply through her nose. "Listen," she says, and my heart pauses. "I need to run use the restroom. Wait right here?"

"I'll stay with him," Sierra says.

Mari nods at her stepsister. "Be right back."

The second Mari jogs out of sight, Sierra turns to me, bounces on her toes, and claps. "Eeee, I can tell Mari has a thing for you."

I run a hand through my hair. "Really?"

"Yes!" Sierra's so excited, she pushes my shoulder. "This is a big deal."

"A big deal?" My voice cracks. "I met her, like, half an hour ago."

Sierra shakes her head. "You don't get it. Mari never dates guys."

"Oh. So she's into girls?"

"No, that's not it. Mari always talks about Shawn Mendes and those guys from BTS, and regrams pictures of pretty much every player on the UT Knoxville football team on her feed. If she was into girls, I'd know it... When I talk about which girls I like, it's not like she joins in."

"Ah. Okay."

"Anyway, Mari likes boys, but doesn't date them."

But she agreed to walk around with me tonight. Why would she do that, if she never goes out with guys? I chew on my lip. I'm into her, but is it worth it to spend a night with her at Lollapalooza, when I could be spending time with my brother, if it's not going to lead anywhere? Not even making out or something?

I shove my hands in my shorts pockets. *Mari doesn't date.* This feels like when the Packers are playing the Patriots, and I know they'll lose before the game even starts. "If she doesn't date, then why do you think she'd suddenly start now, with me, the random guy she met in the Ryde?"

"Seriously?" Sierra exclaims. "Did you see the way Mari was looking at you? She's totally into you, even if she doesn't know it... You're interested in her, right?"

I don't even know her, but there is something there. *Something more* I'd love to explore, if I can, before I go home to Wisconsin and she leaves for Tennessee. Not sure if what I feel is physical or emotional or plain old excitement, or all three, but I do know I want to spend time with Mari tonight.

Still, what's the deal? Why doesn't she like dating? Did some asshole hurt her? I feel a sudden urge to put on my boxing gloves and punch the bag at the gym.

That's when Mari comes back from the bathroom. I notice her lips are a brighter shade of red than before. She put on more makeup. That's a good sign, right?

"Ready?" I ask her.

She sweeps her curly hair back away from her face, glances in my eyes, and nods. "Let's take Sierra to find her friends first, and then we can go to Foo Fighters together."

After making sure Sierra finds her friends, Mari and I walk

toward Tito's stage. This time, I don't make any attempts to take her hand or touch her. I don't want to put any pressure on or suggest I expect something from her.

Tyler would tell me to be cool and relaxed, so that's what I try to do. I shake out my shoulders and tell myself we're going to have a great time.

We join an enormous, cheering audience. Strobe lights flash as people jump up and down, throw their hands in the air, and move their hips to the beat.

I begin to clap and yell "Woooo!"

Mari bounces on her toes, throws a fist up, and goes "Wooooo!" too.

The excitement makes my body buzz with anticipation. I smile down at Mari. Our eyes meet and she swallows.

A guitar screams out, making people go wild. Mari and I clap and cheer, our arms pressed against each other. She begins to dance, and it's so sexy it makes my throat close up. This is it for me. This is how I die. The most gorgeous girl I've ever met murders me with a sway of her hips.

She reaches for both my hands. "Dance with me!"

My worst memory flashes before me. What if Mari rejects me like Lacey did?

I run a hand through my hair, nervously ruffling it. "I'm a terrible dancer," I say over the music.

Her eyes scan me up and down. "Not possible. You're so strong."

My face blushes. "Trust me, it's a one hundred percent

possibility. Actually, it's probably more like a hundred and ten percent."

"Nobody is a terrible dancer. Dancing is just dancing. It's unique to you."

"Then mine is uniquely terrible."

We laugh together, and there's something soft in her eyes that makes me comfortable, that makes me trust her enough to let go. And with the music blasting in the sweltering summer heat, my thoughts go empty as my body takes over, with a mind of its own.

For the first time in my life, I somehow know how to dance. It's so easy and natural, I can't not dance with her. One song after another, we dance and dance, and as the Foo Fighters go deeper into their set, our bodies inch closer and closer together.

It's crowded here, crushed among a thousand people. I move to stand behind Mari. I slip my hands around her waist and rest my chin on her shoulder. "Is this okay?"

She responds by leaning against my chest. We sway back and forth together, and as the sun is setting into oranges and pinks that I desperately want to paint, and the skylight eventually turns to a dark purple, I feel at home.

Under the night sky, the bass thumps along with my heart. Mari dances in a circle, lost in her own beat. Her hips move in a sensual rhythm, giving me all sorts of naughty ideas. Desire builds under my skin.

Summoning all my courage, I reach out to touch her waist, to pull her against my front, to meet her eyes. She tentatively touches my arm. Her fingers skim my skin, giving me goose bumps. I sigh, relieved she hasn't pulled away, happy she's still looking up at me.

Our hands join, our fingers intertwine as if they are one. I can't believe this is happening. Mari grins up at me, biting her lower lip. With a deep breath, I press my forehead to hers.

My blood is on fire.

I bring her hand to my mouth, to kiss her knuckles. Her skin is silk against my lips. I hold my breath, praying she doesn't pull away. Instead she draws closer.

"Hi," I whisper.

"Hi."

My grin feels brighter than the moon. "I'm glad I met you."

She opens her mouth to speak, then closes it.

Then our moment is lost: the band begins playing a fast song and people around us begin to dance and jump. Up and down, up and down. We find ourselves bouncing, too, and it's kind of fun at first, but then people crowd forcefully against us, pinning us in place.

A random guy slams into me, knocking me sideways and away from Mari. Our hands rip apart.

People begin to shout as the crowd smashes together. A man shoves my side as a woman shoves my other arm.

My body moves on its own accord, rushing to get out of here.

Then my brain takes over. I can't run away. Mari's here. Can't leave her.

People scatter. A girl falls to the dirt in front of me. A man trips over her legs. I stop to help the girl to her feet before the crowd crushes her. Where's Mari? Where is she? I spin in a circle.

Grown men knock women down, trying to find a path out. It's a *Lord of the Flies* mosh pit.

"T.J.!" Mari yells as she's being jostled away, swallowed up by the crowd, hands reaching for me.

I push through people, charging her way, but it's like the crowd is multiplying out of thin air. Where are all these people coming from? They continue to bounce. Up, down, up, down.

Suddenly I can't lift my arms. I can't move at all. Sweat beads on my forehead. I edge forward, completely pinned in place. Can't move. Can't move. My breathing races. Heart beats wildly. Who ever thought mosh pits were a good idea?

I could die here. Crushed by strangers.

I frantically look around for Mari. Search for curly dark hair and glasses. I see nothing.

"Mari!" I shout.

Nothing. I hear nothing but other people's cheers.

Why did I let Mari's hand go? I thought I was strong. All that time in the gym didn't help for shit when it really mattered. What kind of man am I?

I continue to push through people in the direction Mari went, searching face by face, but still don't see her. What feels like years later, the crowd begins to even out. I'm no longer trapped.

I bend over, place my hands on my knees, and catch my breath. My heart races like I've been sprinting on a treadmill.

With no sign of Mari, I don't know what else to do. I decide to go to the Perry's sign, where Tyler told me to meet him later.

The crowd is still thick, so I zigzag around people, searching every face for her. Even moving at a rapid pace, it still takes several minutes before the large red and blue Perry's sign comes into view.

I text my brother: Please come to Perry's sign

Tyler: Be right there.

While waiting for him, I lean over onto my knees and breathe.

When Tyler arrives after what feels like a year later, he places a hand on my shoulder. "You okay, man?"

"Ty, I lost Mari. She's gone."

Tyler's eyes sweep the mob of people behind me. "What do you mean she's gone?"

I grab at a tuft of my hair. "I lost her in the crowd. I'm worried she's hurt. It was so crowded in this mosh pit and people fell. What if she got trampled?"

Tyler shakes his phone. "Text her."

I stare down at my screen, knowing it can't help me. "I never got her number."

"Do you think she's okay?"

"I don't know."

I don't know.

Mari

The crowd rips me from T.J.

He reaches out for my arm, but he's too far away.

"T.J.!" I call. The roar of voices drowns my own.

His mouth is moving, trying to tell me something. What's he saying?

A guy steps on my foot. *Shit that hurts.* I push him away from me.

"Bitch," he spits.

Bouncing past, another man accidentally hits my side. I fall to the ground. The right side of my body screams in pain. My elbow burns. My knee is on fire.

I try to stand, but people are crowded too close. I push against them, desperate to climb to my feet.

"Help!" I shout, and a woman beside me and reaches down to help me up.

As I lumber to a stand, my eyes blur. Did I hit my head? My

glasses are lopsided on my face. I push them up my nose, making sure they aren't bent.

"Thank you," I tell the woman, and she nods, then begins to dance and jump again. Being in a mosh pit is not fun at all. I need to get out of here.

My knees are shaking. I can't fall down again—I may not stand back up.

Where's T.J.? My eyes scan the crowd. How did I lose him? He was right here beside me. Holding me.

"T.J.! T.J."

No response.

With one foot after the other, with bodies pressed against me on all sides, I elbow my way out until the crowd begins to thin into small groups of people. I limp toward the vendors set up alongside the edge of the venue. I take a seat on a ledge behind a T-shirt booth. Lights from the city and concert softly illuminate this area, but it's still dark. While this doesn't feel totally safe, it's better than getting squashed into the ground like a bug.

A bunch of roadies are standing around smoking cigarettes. Normally I hate that smell. Tonight, I couldn't care less as long as I can sit here safely.

I take a deep breath to calm down but end up inhaling cigarette smoke and begin to cough.

How bad am I hurt? I stretch my legs out in front of me. Both of my knees are skinned, but the right one is worse. Bits of skin are ripped away, and it's all bloody. My elbow looks much the same. Purple splotches dot my skin. It reminds me of how I used to look when I started Rollerblading in first grade.

Tomorrow I'll be covered in bruises, but at least I'm alive and nothing seems broken. Where's that medical tent Tyler mentioned?

"You okay?"

I glance up to find a man looming above me, taking a deep drag from his cigarette. It glows red in the night.

Could I still do my self-defense moves? My body feels like I've been in a fight with the Hulk. At the moment, I doubt I could even take down Asshole Bob.

"Got somebody you can call?" he asks, tapping his cigarette. Ashes float to the ground.

"Yeah," I say, swiping my phone screen on to text Sierra, only to discover a bunch of messages from her: Where are you? Have you made out with TJ yet? You guys would make such cute babies.

I roll my eyes at her texts.

Me: Meet me at the medical tent

Sierra: OMG are you okay?

Mari: I think so, but need a Band-aid

"Thank you," I tell the man, rising to my feet.

After consulting the festival map on my phone, I make my way to the medical area, where I get into a short line. People from the fire department are providing first aid to the injured.

One lady with tears rolling down her cheeks is clutching her wrist. Another man is holding a compress to his forehead. A guy is hopping on one leg while he waits to be seen.

I glance down at my bloody knees. Looks like I got off easy compared to some people. Lollapalooza is bonkers.

Once I reach the front of the line, a firefighter treats my wounds with antiseptic and covers them with white bandages.

"Mari!" Sierra comes running up and throws her arms around me. "Oh no, you're hurt."

"I'm fine."

She swipes on her cell and says in a matter-of-fact way, "I'll call Mom and David. They can come pick us up."

"No, don't. I'm fine—it's only some scratches and bruises." I gently run a hand over my tender elbow.

"Are you sure?" my stepsister asks.

"I don't want to miss the festival. And if I leave now, I might not find T.J. I may never see him again. I hope he's okay."

Sierra glances around. "Wait. Where is he?"

I look down at my hand. It's still warm from where his was tucked into mine. "We got separated. I never got his number."

Didn't kiss him either.

She gives me a look. "Girl, you should've locked that shit down."

"It's not like I was going to stop dancing to ask for his handle."

Sierra touches my shoulder. "You danced with him? How was it?"

My body tingles just thinking about his body brushing against mine. It felt so good, and if we hadn't been interrupted, I'm not sure how I would have stopped. "Hot. It was hot."

Sierra lifts her eyebrows. "Nice, girl." She holds up her phone. "I'll look him up. What's his last name?"

"I don't know."

"You don't know?"

"No."

Sierra's expression turns stricken. But then she quickly pats my shoulder. "I have an idea! Let's message the Ryde driver."

With quick fingers, I open the rideshare app and begin to type a message.

Hi—my sister and I were in your car with two guys a couple hours ago. Can you give me their contact info?

Hopefully he'll respond. After all, I gave him a good rating and a tip. A few minutes later, the driver messages me back: Can't give personal info of other riders. Company says so.

"That sucks," Sierra says. She starts typing on her phone. I lean over her shoulder, watching as she pulls up Instagram and searches for the name "T.J."

Results pop up on the screen. A ton of them. So many you'd think every guy in the world is called T.J. The name T.J. is the new John.

We scroll through the pictures, looking for anything resembling the cute blond surfer-looking guy I met tonight, but don't see anyone. After Instagram, we try Snapchat, Twitter, and even Facebook.

"Search on Thomas Jefferson," I say, but there is a surprising amount of people with that name too. Besides, isn't Jefferson his middle name? Or maybe it is his full name, and T.J. stands for both his first and last names. Who the hell knows?

Sierra shakes her head. "We need a last name. That's the only way we'll find him on here."

"He said he's from Madison, Wisconsin," I say, and Sierra starts the search all over again and still finds nothing. Maybe his profiles are private so you can't search for him. Maybe he's not online at all, like the few private people from school who claim they hate social media. Honestly, though, I bet they have secret accounts under pseudonyms.

"What bands did he want to see?" she asks.

"He mentioned this one band, If We Were Giants."

Huddled over my phone, we look the band up online and find they aren't playing until Sunday at noon.

"Did he say anything about tonight?" Sierra asks.

"He only mentioned the Foo Fighters concert. That's where we got separated."

"Let's go back over there! Maybe he stayed put. Maybe he's waiting for you!"

T.J.

"She said she wanted to see Shawn Mendes."

I gaze at the huge crowd. There are literally thousands of girls here waiting for Shawn to come onstage. Thousands of girls he could have in a heartbeat.

"What does she look like?" Tyler's friend Mike asks.

"Glasses and dark curly hair. Like, chestnut colored."

"Chestnut?" Tyler gives me a look like he's never heard anything so ridiculous, and I'm reminded why I never talk to him about painting.

"It's all girls here. Tons of them," Mike says, wearing expressions of both awe and horror, as if these women might have their way with him and then eat him alive, praying mantis–style.

Tyler scrubs a hand through his hair. "Man, I don't think we'll find her here. We'll spend all night looking."

I can tell my brother doesn't want to spend his time at the festival helping me find a girl I just met. I need to figure out the quickest way to find Mari, and fast. *Think, T.J. Think.*

With all the weed smoke wafting through the air, thinking is tougher than it should be. I tilt to the side, a bit light-headed.

"Oh, I know," I say. "Let's text the Ryde driver."

Tyler's eyes go askance. "Er... He, uh, may not be happy with me."

"How come?"

"Uhhh... I gave him a one-star rating and, uh, left a comment that he may have permanently damaged my brother's junk."

"He damaged your junk?" Mike asks, his voice suddenly high and squeaky.

"Dude, why'd you do that?" I ask Tyler.

"It's the principle of the thing." He shrugs. "It was a bad ride, so he gets a bad rating."

I rub my eyes. "I thought it was a great ride."

"Who'd you ride?" Tyler's friend Chris walks up, carrying a beer in each hand. He passes one of the beers to Tyler, who takes a generous sip.

"T.J. met this beautiful girl earlier, and we're trying to find her," Tyler explains.

He thinks Mari's beautiful? I don't like that he looked at her that way, but I'm proud he approves.

Tyler goes on, "Teej was totally going to seal the deal with this girl. I know it."

My face blazes hot at Tyler blatantly talking about my sex

life, or lack thereof. It's true, I'd like to sleep with her—I mean, I'd reeeeally like that, but is that even realistic?

Sierra said Mari is perpetually single. Why would she suddenly start with me? On the other hand, she grabbed my hands and started dancing all sexy with me. It was the hottest moment of my life. I need to continue said moment. If she were here, I'd pull her against me. My body suddenly feels all caveman-ish, like *Me Tarzan, You Jane.*

Chris gestures at the crowd with his beer. "Just pick somebody else."

"Yessss," Tyler says.

Chris and Tyler bump fists and chug their beers.

Tyler really thinks I should do that? Go find someone else? I don't want to just pick anyone. I want to find Mari.

I open up Instagram on my phone and type in "Mary" and "Tennessee." A ton of results pop up. I scroll through them, not seeing her picture anywhere. What if Mary isn't her real first name? I search on Maryanne and Maria and Marina and several other possible variations like Mare and Mari and even Marce, which I've never even heard before, but why not?

When I type in Marigold, I've officially lost it. The only girls named Marigold are (1) Disney princesses or (2) three hundred years old. Not my type.

Next, I open Facebook and search again. Nothing. Maybe she has her accounts set to private?

Tyler takes another long sip of beer. "I can't believe you didn't get her number."

"I was going to ask. Just not until later."

"You should've asked for it first thing. Next time, you ask, okay?"

I fight not to roll my eyes. I love my brother, but he doesn't get that he and I aren't the same person. He's the guy who'd strut up a cliff and dive into the ocean. Meanwhile, I would spend, like, ten minutes scoping out the terrain to make sure I wouldn't bust my head open on pointy rocks, before deciding to go back down the cliff, sit on the beach, and draw pictures in the sand.

But if he dared me to jump off the cliff into the water? I probably would.

I worry I'll never live up to everything he's done. My grades and SAT scores weren't as good as his, but I still managed to get into the University of Chicago business program like he did. I'm glad I've done that much at least.

What if I acted more like Tyler outside of school? More confident. The kind of guy who would ask for Mari's number immediately. Maybe I'd be meeting up with her again right now, finishing the dance we started.

"Next time I'll ask first thing," I tell Tyler, not knowing if it's the truth or a lie.

He smiles. "Good. You're a catch, Teej."

Tyler holds up his phone and snaps a selfie of us together, making sure to keep our beers out of the picture, then texts it to Mom.

I watch as she immediately writes back: 😊🖤

Tyler holds his beer cup out to toast with me. I tip my cup

against his and we drink together. As I'm dropping my hand back down, Tyler catches sight of my arm.

"I like those bracelets," he says, pointing at two of the leather cords I made. "I need one of those."

Hearing my brother's compliment feels like the last day of school, because I made these. But I'm not going to tell him. He may like the bracelets, but I can't imagine Tyler Clark would be happy his brother's secret hobby is making jewelry.

"I'll get you some," I say.

"Nice. Thanks, man."

While Tyler's drinking beer and goofing around with Chris and Mike, I take the time to think. How can I find Mari?

I rack my brain, searching my memory for clues. She never told me her last name, but she's from Tennessee. She's traveling... She said she's in town to see Millie Jade.

That's it! I'll go to the Millie Jade show and search until we meet again. It has to be easier finding her there than at Shawn Mendes, who—when it comes to girls—seems to have the gravitational pull of a planet.

I call up the festival schedule on my phone and find Millie Jade isn't playing until Sunday afternoon. Shit. That's two days away. Plus I'm supposed to take the bus home to Wisconsin that night because Tyler has work on Monday morning and needs to sleep. Even if I find her Sunday, there won't be any time left to spend with her.

"Let's think strategically." Tyler raises his beer cup toward the sky. "If you were a girl, where would you go?"

I shrug. "The Shawn Mendes concert?"

My brother shoots me a look.

"Let's check the porta potties," Chris says. "Girls always need to go to the bathroom."

I don't think that's right, but I have no other leads.

That's how I find myself standing outside of a long line of porta potties at Perry's, watching who goes in and out like we're cops waiting for speeding cars. Yeah, this isn't creepy at all.

Tyler, Chris, and Mike don't seem to care where they are, as long as they can drink beer and hear music. I don't mind standing near Perry's stage. The EDM band playing right now is really good. I add the song to a playlist on my phone.

"I don't get it," Chris says. "What's so special about this girl?"

"It just felt right."

"I understand that," Mike replies.

Chris nudges Mike. "You are so whipped, man."

Mike only shrugs and takes another drink from his plastic cup. "When you know, you know."

"Mike's been dating Ashley since sophomore year of college," Tyler explains.

"I don't get how you can lock yourself down like that," Chris says. "I mean, there are so many choices."

It seems gross that Chris is saying this as we're watching women beside the porta potties. Though, a lot of my friends back home would agree with Chris—that it doesn't matter who you're with as long as you can fool around.

But I don't believe that. My brother was right when he said to find a girl who makes my blood catch fire. Then I'd know what to do. Everything tonight felt so natural with Mari.

I don't want to give that chance up.

"I'm worried about her," I say. "What if she got hurt in that mosh pit?"

Tyler squeezes my shoulder. "If she's hurt, I imagine she left and went home."

I nod, hoping she's okay.

"I think we've looked enough here," Tyler says. "Let's go back to the Foo Fighters, okay?"

Mari

With no luck at the Foo Fighters concert, Sierra and I make our way back to the Shawn Mendes show.

When we meet up with her group of friends, literally twenty different girls crowd around us, wanting to inspect my injuries and hear how I got caught in a mosh pit and fell.

"You must've been terrified," her friend Megan shouts to me over the music.

"Oh, she was!" Sierra says, and then she tells Megan the whole story as if it happened to her.

Depending on who Sierra's talking to in her group, she easily switches from Spanish to English and back to Spanish again. When she's speaking Spanish, the only thing I understand is "T.J."

I wish I could speak another language like Sierra. My stepmother, Leah, sent her to a Spanish immersion school when she was growing up, and now she's at a bilingual high school, learning in both English and Spanish. Leah told her that knowing a foreign language is one of the most important things you can do for your future. I believe it. Sierra definitely uses Spanish frequently.

When I heard my dad was remarrying, I automatically figured I'd hate my new family, because that's what happens in the movies, but nobody could dislike Sierra. I've always admired how friendly she is, how she manages to move from group to group and fit right in.

The moment we met, she sat me down and asked question after question, wanting to learn all about me. She was open with me too, being up front that she's bi. Coming from a conservative town and high school where hardly anybody is out, it made me happy to know my stepsister trusted me with her truth.

My parents' divorce was the worst thing that ever happened to me, but meeting Sierra was one of the best.

"So you don't know how to find T.J.?" one of Sierra's friends asks. I don't know her name.

"No clue," I say.

"You've already searched online?"

"Obviously," Sierra says, then begins speaking in rapid Spanish to one of her other friends. The entire time she's talking, she's keeping an eye on Megan.

Megan is Black, has gorgeous braids, including some pinks and purples, and is wearing a sporty camo halter dress and a thick set of combat boots.

"Why are you wearing those?" I ask her. "It's so hot out here."

"Better for mosh pits than sneakers," she tells me.

That must be why T.J. wore them. It makes me feel like a music festival noob.

I don't know Megan well—this is the first time we've met, but I see her on Sierra's IG all the time. They make funny videos together, doing everything from dance routines to filming pranks. They did this one where they pretended to eat mayo right out of the jar in front of the boys' basketball team in the cafeteria. The boys screamed because they were so grossed out, but Megan had swapped the mayo for vanilla pudding.

My stomach rumbles. I never ate dinner. Wait, didn't T.J. say he couldn't wait for deep-dish? Maybe he's as hungry as I am.

Hoping to find T.J., we go to the Lou Malnati's pizza stand to buy slices. While we wait in line, Sierra's friends dance to the music. Sierra and Megan start doing naughty moves, which cracks us all up.

Once I've ordered and received my slice, I take a bite of the deep dish and end up liking the gooey cheese more than I thought I would. As I stand there eating, hoping he'll show up, I have a chance to check out the crowd. And boy am I sorry I looked. Two men in line for pizza appear to be snorting cocaine. A guy eating a slice of pizza is wearing a Speedo—and only a Speedo.

A young couple is making out. They kiss the entire time we're eating our pizza. What's the world record for kissing? When they finally pull away from each other for a break, Sierra starts cheering and we join in. The drunk couple appears confused by our applause, but then they start laughing and take a bow.

I'm cracking up, but I'm envious at how comfortable they seem with each other. I did miss out on kissing T.J. I can't believe I lost him before I had a chance to start a hot summer fling like in a rom-com. Sigh.

"I really thought T.J. might show up here," I say.

"I have an idea!" Sierra begins tapping on her phone. She pulls up a photo of T.J. and me from earlier. I didn't even know she had taken a picture. Sierra must've snapped it while we were waiting in line to get into the concert.

In the photo, the sky behind us is a soft pink and purple, a cotton candy swirl. I'm pushing my hair behind an ear and smiling down at the ground. My glasses are embarrassingly perched on the tip of my nose. Still, T.J. is gazing at me like I'm made of gold.

My stomach leaps into my throat.

Megan peeks around Sierra's other shoulder. "Oh, Mari, he's hot. You guys are so cute together. You're my life goals."

"Life goals? Like, making enough money to go on tropical vacations?"

"You know, *life* goals," Megan says, looking from me to Sierra. "Finding true love."

True love? I'd only met T.J. about twenty minutes before that picture was taken. Besides, while my life goals do include kissing and hopefully not dying a virgin, they don't include finding true love. That sounds like something out of a fairy tale, not real life. When I think about couples from school—even the ones I swore would be together forever, nearly all of them break up at some point or another.

The idea of love only goes so far.

Sierra smiles sideways at me. "Okay, you guys. Get ready to retweet me."

She opens Twitter, uploads the picture, and types: At #Lollapalooza tonight with my sister Mari who met T.J. earlier but lost him in the crowd. Anybody know him? Help us find him! #WhenMariMetTJ #FindTJforMariPleeeeeease

All the girls take out their phones and retweet the post.

On my own screen, I stare at the picture again. It's kind of hard not to. I can't get over how deeply T.J. is gazing at me, how happy I look. The photo feels like hope on Christmas morning, when you wake up and rush to unwrap presents under the tree, searching for the gift you wanted most. My skin flushes with desire. I can't believe I missed out on the chance to make out with him.

I'm here all weekend. If only I can find him ...

I doubt any of my Twitter followers will be linked to T.J.'s life, but it's worth a shot. I push the retweet button in hopes someone will see it and connect us.

Our group decides to go back to the Shawn Mendes concert while waiting to see if the tweet works. One of Sierra's friends who has a fake ID passes a couple of beers around and we take sips, laughing.

As we're dancing, Sierra flicks her phone screen on. "I've

already got three hundred retweets! Of course my most popular tweet ever wouldn't even be about my own love life," she pouts.

I nudge her. "Hey, you could've gone for it. You're the one who forced me to sit beside him in the car."

She blows me an air kiss. "You love me."

"I do."

Sierra leans against me sideways. "I wish you'd come visit more often... I missed you."

Her words bring tears to my eyes. Even though we text all the time, this is only the third time I've ever hung out with Sierra. I came for Dad's wedding to his new wife two years ago and then once last summer to visit. Meanwhile, he's never come back to visit me.

"It's hard," I tell my stepsister. "It makes my mom sad when I come here—she gets jealous if I'm with y'all."

"That really sucks." Sierra stops dancing and slips her arm into mine, walking me farther away from the music so we can talk.

"I feel caught between my parents," I tell her. "Mom didn't want me to come this weekend. She, like, screamed and cried at me, and begged me not to come."

Sierra's eyebrows furrow. "Have you told David any of this? He thinks you just don't want to visit."

"I want to visit *you*," I say. But my dad? My feelings are complicated. I love him—I like him even, but I hate what he did. It's hard to get past that. I don't know if I ever will.

"He hasn't even made an effort to come see me," I start,

"and I'm the one who has to live with my mom. She's always so angry." Purple and green lights from the stage illuminate Sierra's face. She's watching me closely as I talk over the loud music. "Mom is going to freak out when I get home, and Dad won't have to deal with any of it because he's gone."

I wish I were gone from Tennessee, too, but I have an entire year before college. I've been giving thought to the University of Chicago, because it has a great physics program, it's close to Sierra, and like I said, I love this city.

I go back and forth on whether I should ask Dad if I could live with him while I'm in school, to save money on a dorm. But it would make things worse with Mom. Dad already left her. If I left, too, and came here to college and lived with Dad, would she lose it?

I bet she would.

A big part of me wants to ask Dad if I can move to Chicago now, to get away from Mom and her temper. Nobody knows how bad things get sometimes.

I stare down at my phone, flicking through my notifications to make sure I haven't missed any texts. "Mom hasn't even checked to make sure I arrived safely. She must be super pissed at me."

Sierra looks taken aback. "My mom's already texted me four times since we've arrived at this concert."

"Well, your mom is normal," I snap, then immediately regret my tone. "I'm sorry."

"You don't have to apologize to me. We're family."

Family. It's so nice to have someone in my corner.

When I was little I thought family meant a group of people with an unbreakable bond. People who would be there, no matter what. Family came together, so it would stay together. So fucking naïve.

I worried my coming here would send Mom into an emotional tailspin, like the time she flipped out when Leah and Sierra sent me a new jacket for Christmas. A jacket Mom can't afford. When I opened the package and squealed with happiness, she ripped the jacket out of my hand and threw it on the floor, with no regard for my happiness or consideration for Leah and Sierra's kindness. I understood why she felt so hurt and upset, but that didn't make her actions okay.

That was the worst Christmas Eve ever.

The entire night, I kept picturing Dad with his new family, sitting around the Christmas tree, eating cookies and listening to music, while I was listening to Mom scream and cry about how she didn't want to be alive anymore.

It scared me so much, I called my aunt Gina to come over and help, but that pissed Mom off even more. She saw what I did as a betrayal. She didn't want anyone—not even her sister—to see her at such a low point.

Aunt Gina convinced Mom to try therapy. She went once, but never again. Mom said she didn't need therapy, and she couldn't risk her women's church group finding out about it. She forbade me from ever calling her sister again either.

The fallout from this trip to Chicago has the potential to be equally as terrible as that Christmas Eve—what if Mom says she wants to die again?

But I need to see Millie Jade sing in person. Seeing her will help me sort my life out. Put things into perspective. Maybe even help me figure out my destiny.

"Thanks again for inviting me," I tell Sierra. "I never would've thought to try to see Millie Jade in person."

She pats my hand. "You should do things for yourself like this more often."

"That's hard when I feel like the only adult... Dad wants stuff from me. Mom wants stuff from me. And then they get pissed when I agree with the other. It's still hard to believe they got divorced. I never saw it coming."

It's not something I like thinking about. Back when I was eleven, Mom got pregnant with a baby boy, but she ended up losing him at six months. It devastated her. After that, Mom couldn't get close to Dad again. It was like something snapped in her. She didn't want him touching her. Not even a hug. She could barely look at him.

Since she wouldn't let Dad touch her, they drifted apart. Even though they were still together, living together physically, Dad had moved on mentally. But he should've tried to help more—offered to get counseling. Asked for help at our church. Anything. Instead he retreated inside himself, just like Mom did.

He ended up meeting Leah online a couple years later. I remember screaming at him, I was so pissed that he met someone on the internet. In a Marvel fansite, of all places. And worse, he cheated on Mom with her. He said he'd done it because he was lonely and needed someone to talk to.

Next thing I knew, he'd decided to leave Tennessee and move to Chicago.

It's hard not to resent both of my parents, but like I said, I'm the adult here.

"Mari, there's a bunch of responses to Sierra's tweet!"

Megan rushes over to us, her thumb scrolling on her phone.

I pull up Twitter on my screen, praying someone's tagged T.J. so we can find each other. My smile melts as I sort through the responses. Some of them are totally mean.

One random lady wrote: Forget Mari, come find me TJ! She's a 6, you a 10.

Another person tweeted: Think I saw him in Times Square. Better hurry there quick!

How stupid. We're in Chicago, not New York. A bunch of people have already written back to that commenter, telling them what's what.

But there are fun responses too:

Hope you find each other!

So cute. Fingers crossed you find him! I can tell TJ's in lovvveee! #WhenMariMetTJ

Love? I examine the look on T.J.'s face in the picture. He does seem into me—maybe more into me than I am to him. There's lust, maybe. But love? This weekend is supposed to be fun and simple. Love is messy and complicated and unnecessary.

Why do you need another person to be happy?

T.J.

With no sign of Mari, I'm not sure what else to do besides try to enjoy the concert.

We head back to Tito's, where the crowd has started the biggest mosh pit I've ever seen. After getting caught in that mosh pit earlier, the idea of being smashed between all those people freaks me out, so we stay toward the back where we can still hear the music and dance.

My brother sneaks me a beer. "I'm glad you came out with us. We'll have to hang out when you move here for college."

I nod with a smile and sip from my plastic cup. The beer tastes bitter, but also cool and crisp in this billion-degree weather. I could get used to this.

Tyler leans near my ear and says over the music, "Try to have fun tonight, okay?"

My brother's four years older than me, so we've never been particularly close. He was always ahead of me. I was playing T-ball when he was a Little League star. When I was in middle school, he was preparing to graduate from high school and leave home.

Sure, we played video games a lot growing up and fought over the last piece of bread at the supper table, but not much beyond that. We didn't go to the movies or hang out with our friends together. We were too far apart.

It means a lot he's willing to see me as an equal now, as someone worthy of hanging out with. He invited me to this concert because he wanted to spend time with me. Yeah, I want to find Mari, but I also don't want to be the shitty one who whines throughout the whole concert about a girl.

As Tyler and Chris approach a group of girls, I want to stand with Mike, who's more focused on the music, probably because he has a girlfriend. But one of the girls is looking over at me expectantly. My brother beckons me to stand next to him. Tyler's never going to ask me to go out again if I mope around.

With a deep breath, I scrub a hand through my hair and move to his side.

A small blond with a pixie cut gives me a coy smile as she sips from her beer.

Chris leans around the back of Tyler to talk to me. "Man, you gotta go for it with this one. She's into you."

Is Chris right? Should I pick somebody random and just do it already? I'm sick of getting myself off.

Before I can even say hi to the girl who's supposedly into me, things around me begin to escalate. It's like I suddenly entered a raunchy nightclub.

This one lady starts doing these dirty grinding moves against Tyler. He seems really into it. Jesus. No one wants to see their brother practically making a fully clothed porno.

At the same time, another woman pours alcohol on her chest and Chris does a body shot off her skin. Then Tyler rips off his shirt, screams "Wooo!", pours beer on his own chest, and two girls do body shots off him.

Mike is recording the whole thing on his phone while laughing his ass off. Being totally nosy, I watch as he posts the video to IG, tagging two handles I don't recognize. One of the handles is @ChrisdaLadiesMan, and the other is @T-Bonezzz.

T-Bonezzz?

Does Tyler have a secret IG account?

His Instagram, the one I follow, is a bunch of pictures of him looking important wearing a suit, going to Cubs games, lifting weights, and petting our dog. There certainly aren't any videos of him doing body shots. I mean, I can understand why. Can you get a job at a hedge fund if you call yourself T-Bonezzz, chug beer, and do the Running Man dance while people cheer you on?

I don't even want to know what T-Bonezzz means.

I'm not going to do body shots or dirty dance, but I guess I can talk to this girl. It's the polite thing to do, even though I'd rather be talking to Mari.

I stick out my hand to the blond with the pixie cut. "Hi, I'm T.J."

"I'm Dawn."

_____

I'm trying to pay attention to Dawn, the girl I just met, but that's impossible when your brother has started a drunken conga line.

A. Drunken. Conga. Line.

The last time I saw a conga line was at my cousin Joel's wedding when I was in eighth grade. Grandma Pat started a conga line and everybody above the age of thirty joined in. Meanwhile, Tyler led a group of older kids out onto the deck to drink the bottles of wine he had nicked. I spied on them and listened as they made fun of the adults for doing the conga.

And now he's doing it himself? He claps his hands above his head and turns in a wide circle, and his entire conga line of like twenty people copies him.

Only Tyler could make the conga seem cool.

"Where are you from?" I shout to Dawn over the music.

"Here!" She starts to dance with me, and I try—I really do, but I feel like my arms are moving like an octopus's tentacles. I hope nobody's watching me. Why can't I just act normal? Why can't I dance with her like I did with Mari earlier? I try to replicate the moves I did with my hips before. This time, I probably look like one of those flailing tube man balloons at a used car dealership.

Dawn gives me a weird look. Without a word, she moves on to another guy in the crowd, dancing uninhibitedly like no one is watching.

My face burns in embarrassment. Yeah, I wasn't all that

interested in her, but I didn't expect her to ditch me a few lines into a song. Why do I always screw up with girls?

Tyler breaks from his line and congas over to me. "What happened? Where'd she go?"

"I guess I suck at dancing."

My brother lifts an eyebrow. "You're a Clark. You were born to dance!" He pats my chest. "Have confidence, Teej."

Tyler has been saying that a lot lately. But saying it doesn't seem to do shit. I still feel like the same person. The same weak guy who let go tonight when Mari was ripped out of my arms.

With my beer in hand, I walk back over to where Mike is standing listening to the music. We sing along to the song together. Out of the corner of my eye, I see Dawn approach my brother to dance. I gasp.

He shakes his head hard at her, then turns around and ignores her.

I'm glad he said no, but I hate always being an afterthought. With him as a big brother, how could I be anything but?

Tyler is double fisting two beers. He hands one to me.

"I had the best idea while I was waiting in line," he says, taking a long sip from his cup.

I drink too. The crisp taste is really growing on me. "What's your idea?"

He throws his free arm around my shoulders. "Let's get tattoos."

For once, that's something Tyler and I agree on. "Yes, we should get tattoos."

"That's what I was thinking! Tattoos."

I crack up. "You're the one who brought it up, man." Drunk Tyler is also a hilarious Tyler. "What kind of tattoo do you want?"

"A hula girl." He points at his forearm with his beer cup. "Right here. That would look so legit at the gym. You can get one too."

"Not a hula girl." I'm opening my mouth to tell Tyler about my tattoo design I came up with, wondering if he'll approve, when my smartwatch buzzes on my wrist. A text from my best friend, Ethan, lights up the screen:

Who is she?!

I pull my phone from my pocket to reply one-handed.

Huh?

Right then, two younger girls appear in front of me, both wearing Shawn Mendes shirts.

One of them gawks at me. "Oh my God, it's him!"

The other bounces up and down. "It's T.J.!"

Suddenly even more girls surround me, talking and pointing their phones my way. What in the hell is going on? Did I suddenly transform into Shawn Mendes?

Someone jostles my beer and it spills onto my boots with a splash.

I jerk my head around looking for my brother. He and his friends are standing there like deer in the headlights, shocked by the attention I'm getting. Then Chris raises his beer cup and says, "Oh my God, it's T.J.!"

My brother and his friends crack up.

More girls hurry over. Some are in high school, or maybe even college. Tyler's mouth is gaping open. He holds his phone up in my direction. Is he recording me for his secret T-Bonezzz account?

As I'm trying to figure out what's happening, I hear girls saying "Twitter" and "hashtag" and "such a cute picture."

"This is really your night, Teej," Chris calls out. "Can you play wingman for me next?"

"He's my wingman," Tyler retorts. "We're gettin' hula girl tattoos."

I pray that once Tyler's sober, he's forgotten about his tattoo plans. Or at least come up with something better than a hula girl.

Mike pushes through the crowd surrounding me and holds up his phone. "Is this her? The one you're looking for?"

A picture of Mari and me fills his screen. My heart races at the sight of her cute glasses and that bouncy curly brown hair.

Does that say ten thousand retweets?! I scan the Twitter caption to discover she's searching for me too. She's looking for me!

I throw my fist toward the sky and yell, "Wooo!"

The crowd of girls around me whoops too.

I turn on my phone screen to find Ethan texted me back: The girl in that tweet. Mari? Who is she?

I'll have to text him later. For now, I need to find her.

The girls circle me, all talking at once.

A middle schooler wearing a Shawn Mendes shirt snaps at me: "What are you waiting for?"

"Let's go find Mari!" another says.

A girl raises an imaginary sword like we're going to war. "C'mon!"

And suddenly I find myself being bustled away from Tyler by a sea of Shawn Mendes fans.

Mari

My phone buzzes.

And buzzes. And buzzes again. Everybody, their mom, and their grandma—*especially the grandmas*—has retweeted Sierra's tweet, and I'm getting all the notifications. Sierra has been retweeted more than eleven thousand times and liked twenty-four thousand times. In less than an hour.

I think it's because Chrissy Teigen—Chrissy fucking Teigen—retweeted it. It's hard to sort out all the responses, because so many people have been responding and interacting with other people on the thread—mostly arguing over whether I'm good enough for T.J. I can't believe how many people think I need to ditch my glasses and get contacts already. Assholes.

I use my thumb to scroll and scroll through the tweets. Even if he does see Sierra's tweet and reach out to me, will I see his response in all this noise?

While Sierra dances with Megan, I scan hundreds of messages.

That's when I see it.

Kitten_45: Found him!

Along with her message, there's a picture of T.J. standing with Tyler. They're drinking and laughing together. I scan the background to see if I can figure out where they are, but there's nothing discerning about their location: they're in a crowd at Lollapalooza.

I write back: Where did you see him?

But Kitten doesn't respond.

Another message pops up.

TandraM2005: We have TJ at back of Rosalía concert!

This feels like finding a clue in a treasure hunt. "Sierra! Megan! C'mon!"

With the girls on my heels, we make our way through the crowd pushing our way around people. Someone steps on my foot, but I ignore the pain and keep going.

"Mari! Mari!"

A bunch of girls are chanting my name, as if I'm famous. This is the strangest thing that's ever happened to me. I follow murmurs of my name until I come across a crowd of girls surrounding a guy. A very cute guy.

There he is. T.J.

My eyes find his, and he breaks into a big smile. I sprint his way, zigzagging around people. When I reach him, he throws himself into my arms.

People cheer for us so loudly you'd think I was Rosalía herself.

He squeezes and lifts me up, turning me in a circle. At first I'm tense, because I don't know him all that well, and it's a little strange he's holding me so tight. But at the same time, we make complete sense: my body's tingling all over. It feels just right.

"I'm so, so sorry," he says.

"For what?" I say into his ear, so he can hear me over the music.

He gently lowers me to the ground but doesn't release his hold on me. "I let you go. Your hand—I couldn't hold on."

I touch his arm. "It's okay, we found each other."

"Are you all right?" He steps back to examine me. His eyes catch on my bandaged elbow. His fingers gently touch the edge of it. "You're hurt."

"It's nothing serious."

He begins to grin. "I'm so glad Sierra took that picture of us... But in case I lose you again, I have some questions. What's your phone number? What's your IG handle? And is your name Marigold?"

T.J.

"Marigold?"

She looks at me like I have tentacles.

"No. It's just Mari. Mari with an I. Mari Morgan."

"Oh. I'm T.J. Clark."

"Marigold?" she exclaims.

I shrug. "I tried all sorts of names when I was searching online. I couldn't find you."

She takes a step closer, her body flush against mine. "You were looking online for me?"

"There was no way I wouldn't." The tips of my boots touch her sneakers. I wrap my arm around her waist. She fits perfectly against me.

Strangers watching squeal and hoot for us.

"I'm sorry we didn't get to hang out tonight," she says. "I have to leave soon. Dad wants us home by eleven."

I inhale a deep breath, pushing her hair behind an ear, then lean down, letting my lips linger on her neck. She shivers in my arms, even though it's a steaming hot sauna outside.

"I'm sorry too," I reply. "How long are you in town?"

"I have to go home Sunday night. My flight to Nashville is at seven thirty."

I pull back to look at her, but keep my arms around her waist. "That's when I'm taking the bus back to Madison. This sucks. I can't believe we lost this entire night."

Should I ask her to hang out again? Is it worth it? When I lost her tonight and we were separated, I felt terrible, and I'd only known her for less than two hours.

How bad would it feel if I spent the weekend getting to know her, only to lose her? She's leaving for home in two days and I'm going to college in a few weeks. I mean, why get my hopes up that there could be something between us when it will end quickly?

"Want to try again tomorrow?" she asks, before I've even made up my mind about what happens next. There are serious barriers between us: I'm going to college and she's still in high school back in Tennessee.

Besides, Sierra said Mari doesn't go out with guys.

But the hopeful look on Mari's face is what gets me. That's when I decide to go for it.

"We could meet for breakfast," I say.

She stands taller, balancing up onto her tiptoes. "And then go to the beach?"

"And then get hula girl tattoos!" a voice says.

I look over my shoulder to find Tyler has arrived, and he's grinning at me from ear to ear. I return his smile.

And as I lean down to give her another hug, I've never felt more alive.

Mari

Unlike earlier today, it's only Sierra and me in the back of a beige sedan.

It's being driven by a redheaded woman in her twenties who is totally focused on the busy Friday-night traffic, both hands firmly clutching the steering wheel. She doesn't even have the radio on.

"This blows," Sierra mumbles to me. "We should've done the rideshare option again."

"No way, it's late," I reply. "Who knows what kind of wackos might get in the car with us?"

"It could be a wacko, but what if it was, like, a princess in disguise?"

"A princess in disguise?"

Sierra sits up straight and talks with her hands. "Yeah, an undercover princess from Sweden who's in the United States to go to college, and she wants to be normal, so she doesn't tell anyone she's a princess. And then she and I meet in the rideshare, just like you and T.J. She doesn't tell me she's a princess at first, but over time she begins to trust me and then opens up about who she truly is."

"And then you get married and become Princess Sierra?"

My stepsister pumps her fist. "Life goals."

The Ryde rolls to a stop in front of Dad's Gold Coast apartment building. We climb out and circle through the revolving glass door into the lobby.

"Hey, Jason!" Sierra calls out to the concierge, a guy who looks Dad's age.

He smiles and nods back at her. "Good evening, Ms. Lavigne."

Once we're on the elevator, I let out a long yawn, which makes Sierra yawn, and then we're both laughing as we spill out onto my dad's floor. Sierra uses her key fob to unlock the front door to her apartment. Even though it's my dad's place, and I want to stay here when I'm in college, I don't know if I could ever get used to saying "our" apartment. It's not my home. I have my own room in our duplex back in Tennessee, but without Dad there, it doesn't feel like home either.

The apartment door swings open, revealing the long hallway with the fancy tiled floors and lush patterned carpet that looks like it came from the Middle East. When I step onto the rug, my dirty sneakers sink gently into it. The air smells faintly of polish and popcorn. This place is fancy yet cozy, and I simultaneously hate and covet it.

Sierra toes her dirty sneakers off, so I do the same, and leave them by the front door.

"Hello?" Leah's voice calls out.

I take a deep breath. I wish I could go straight to bed, crawl under the covers, and ignore my dad and stepmother, but that won't fly.

Sierra leads me into the living room, where Dad and Leah are curled up together on the couch watching *Iron Man* for probably the zillionth time. A bottle of wine, empty glasses, and a half-eaten bowl of popcorn sit on the coffee table.

Sierra grabs a handful of popcorn, flops down next to her mother on the couch, and leans against her side. I stare. I can't remember the last time I cuddled with my mom. I must've been seven or eight? I can't even imagine simply hugging my parents. It's not something we do.

"How was the concert, Ladybug?" Dad asks me.

"Good," I say quietly.

His eyebrows pinch together. "What's wrong?"

Seeing him happy with his new wife is hard to look at. I'm glad he's found what he was looking for and that he seems comfortable in this new life, but it sucks he left us behind. Resentment bubbles inside me.

"I'm tired," I say. "It's been a long day, with the flight and festival and all."

Leah gives me a kind smile. "I have the guest room all ready for you."

The guest room, because God forbid Dad set up a room for

me at his place. He'd probably say he hasn't because I spend very little time here, but maybe I don't spend time here because I don't have my own space.

"I put some towels in there," Leah goes on. "Let me know if you need anything else."

"May I have some water?"

Her forehead crinkles. "Of course. Feel free to help yourself to anything in the kitchen. Our home is your home."

Is it though?

"Thanks," I say.

Sierra climbs to her feet, popping a couple more pieces of popcorn into her mouth. "C'mon. I'll show you where the glasses are."

After getting a drink and washing my face, I put on my pajamas. In the guest room, I turn off the overhead light, leaving the small bedside lamp on. I climb into bed. Ugh, of course the sheets would be soft and cool. Does everything around here have to be so goddamned perfect?

I swipe on my phone screen to discover I have hundreds of notifications and texts. I'm too tired to sort through it all tonight. Instead I pull up the picture of T.J. and me from earlier.

I don't even look like myself. My skin is glowing and my eyes are bright. I look so happy.

When I turn my focus to T.J.'s picture, my heart speeds up simply looking at him. Would a kiss from him lead to spontaneous combustion?

Once I've had my fill of staring at him, I flick over to the phone app—something I so rarely use I don't even keep the icon on my home screen—and tap on Mom's number. I hold my breath as it dials and rings a few times. Of course it goes to voicemail. She hates talking on the phone as much as I do, but I figured she'd at least want to make sure I arrived okay and that I've settled in.

Part of me is pissed she's avoiding my call; the other is relieved she didn't pick up. I'd have to tap-dance around talking about Dad and Leah and how happy they seem to be. The last thing I need is for Mom to be even more upset about my visit here than she is already is. Whenever she gets mad at me, my nerves crackle like I've been zapped by lightning.

I leave a message: "Hi, Mom, it's me. I'm at Dad's, and I'm okay. Call me back when you have a chance."

Next I flick over to the video messenger and pull up Austin's name. Today's been so overwhelming, I want to see his familiar face—someone who understands. I press the button to call him.

He answers, and his face appears on my screen. "Hey, Bud."

It's nice to hear him call me Bud. That's what he's called me for years. It makes me feel like things could be normal between us again one day. "Hey, yourself."

In the video, he's standing outside in the dark, wearing his usual black cowboy hat. Behind him are a roaring bonfire and a bunch of people tailgating on pickup trucks.

"Am I interrupting anything?" I ask.

Austin looks over his shoulder. "Just hanging out at Goose Pond. You having a good time up there in the city?"

I lean back against the pillows in the guest bed. "Yeah, I mean, it's weird seeing my dad, and it's awkward staying with him."

"I'm sorry. You doing okay?"

"Yeah, I'll be fine," I reply, because it's the only thing to say. Isn't that they way of life? *Everything sucks, but you keep on moving.*

Austin takes off his cowboy hat to push a hand through his dark hair. He looks away from the screen. Awkward.

Awkward is what our friendship has been like the past couple months. It would be nice to have one not-totally-weird relationship in my life. I need a kitten.

"So you met a guy today?" Austin finally says.

I hesitate before answering. Will my answer make my best friend sad or mad or flat out pissed? "Yeah. His name's T.J. He was nice."

"Good."

Good? What does that mean? How can one little word from Austin nearly give me a coronary?

"You going to see him again?" Austin asks.

My hands are shaking I'm so nervous and worried about Austin's reaction. "Yes, tomorrow for breakfast."

Again, Austin musses his hair. He looks down at the ground. The camera wobbles.

"I hope you'll give him a chance," Austin says.

"What do you mean?"

He looks up into my eyes. He opens his mouth, then closes it again.

"Yo, Evans, we're about to start," a girl calls from off-screen. "We've got some ass to kick!"

Austin puts his cowboy hat back on. "I gotta go. We're playing capture the flag. Talk to you later."

The screen goes black and a little survey screen pops up with a message: How was the quality of your call?

The video quality was five stars—it was like I was right back there in Tennessee sitting across from him, but the call content was a one. Austin looked so disappointed. And I hate what he said about me giving T.J. a chance. It was clearly a dig about how I didn't want a relationship with him. He's still upset about what happened between us, but does he have to knock me down?

What did I do to deserve that?

It's after midnight when somebody knocks on the guest room door.

I flop my head on the pillow and pretend to be asleep, but then Sierra pokes her head inside.

She scurries over and plops down on the bed with the popcorn bowl. She must've nicked it from her mom. "Tonight was great."

"It was," I say quietly. Then I plummeted from this wild adrenaline high, crashing back into the real world.

She holds out the bowl to me. "You sure you're okay?"

I choose a piece of popcorn and chew it slowly. "Was it weird when my dad moved in with you guys?"

Sierra nods. "Totally. It was always just me and my mom up until then. And suddenly there was this guy around hogging the orange juice and taking up all Mom's attention... It was annoying at first, but it's getting better, I guess. David's helping me try to convince Mom to adopt a dog, which is good. And now he knows never to touch the last cinnamon roll or he'll face my wrath."

I glance at Sierra's face for a second, but then look away. "You've never met your dad, right?"

"Nope." Sierra busily crunches on the popcorn. "Don't even know his name."

Based on Sierra's tall, strong body, I imagine her dad is an Olympic rower or possibly even an NBA star. When she and I were getting to know each other, she told me over text that by the time Leah was in her late thirties, she wanted a baby, but didn't have a husband or boyfriend, so she used a donor to conceive her. I guess she didn't find anyone until she met my dad online.

I want to talk to Sierra about how Dad cheated on Mom with her mother, but it's too painful, thinking of the day I came home from school to find Mom bawling because Dad had left her to go meet another woman in Chicago. It's hard for me to think of Dad and Leah's happiness when it's brought such major suckage for Mom and me.

I sit up straighter against the pillows. "You know how you said it was weird when Dad moved in with y'all? I feel that way being here."

Sierra picks another piece of popcorn. "Being here's weird for you?"

"I feel so many things... It's hard to sort out." It's like my brain is a flashing screen, jumping from one emotion to the next. It's like a calculus problem I can't work out, and I *hate it* when I can't solve a problem. "I'm sad. Angry...happy because I get to be here with you."

"Aw, you too." Sierra leans her head on my shoulder. "I'm sorry things are weird, but I'm here."

"Thank you," I say, feeling a rush of gratitude for her.

I also feel guilt. So much guilt. Part of me wanted to sit down and chat with Dad and Leah and pretend that Mom isn't waiting for me back home. I want to feel safe and comfortable and just *be* for once.

But even that doesn't seem possible. Not after everything that's happened.

I miss the nights where I'd sit with Dad and work on a puzzle or play cards or do whatever really. I'll never get that back. Even if we do some random activity, it won't feel the same. Going forward, there will always be an asterisk next to our relationship.

How can I ever forgive him for cheating?

As my eyes start to water, Sierra looks up at me. "Are you still hungry?"

"Always."

"C'mon. I made Mom buy us the stuff for hot fudge sundaes."

Now that Dad and Leah have gone to bed, Sierra and I take over the kitchen, laughing and talking and generally making a huge mess of ice cream toppings, getting sprinkles and chocolate chips all over the counter as we fill our ice cream glasses to the rim.

Once our sundaes are made, Sierra raises hers in a toast to me. "To sisters!"

As our glasses clink together, a huge grin takes over my face. "To sisters."

SATURDAY

Mari

My alarm clock wakes me at eight o'clock on Saturday morning. Normally I would never deign to get out of bed this early on a weekend, but not today.

Today I'm meeting T.J.

Before I climb out of bed, I push my AirPods into my ears. Millie Jade is my go-to music in the morning. Her songs—especially "Destiny"—always make me think about how I'm small, but ultimately an important part of something in this big world. I only wish I could figure out my place in it.

As I lie here listening to the song, I picture myself living here while I'm in college. The guest bedroom has maroon flowered wallpaper and heavy oak furniture with ornate carvings. Total grandma furniture. Not my style whatsoever. But I'd deal with it if I could live in Chicago and go to college here.

Before he died, my poppy left me money in a bank account for college. There's not a whole lot there—I'd definitely have to take out student loans, but I should be able to make it work. Paying for room and board would add a lot to the price tag, though. It doesn't make sense to take out a loan to pay for a room if I can avoid it.

Would Dad and Leah even be willing to give up their guest bedroom for me? Leah seems to like everything in its place.

In my earbuds, Millie Jade sings her line, "Destiny always comes back around."

To me, it means that whatever is meant to happen will happen, and nothing can change destiny. I rub my eyes. Nothing is going to change Mom. Her experiences have shaped her, and there's no going back in time to alter them. She is who she is.

There are days when everything is great with her. She'll suggest going out for lunch at Niko's, and she'll spend the whole time chatting with me about whatever, just having a good time.

When she acts loving, it gives me this false sense of security, that everything is finally okay. But then a couple days later, she'll explode for no reason.

Since Dad's not around, she takes her anger at him out on me.

When I asked to visit Chicago this weekend, she literally lost it. She grabbed me by the ponytail and yanked me backward. Tears of pain and humiliation and resentment and being just plain fed up rushed to my eyes.

She'd never hurt me physically like that before.

When she yells, I don't know what she expects me to say.

How she expects me to make things better. I don't have any power to help. I can't change what happened with Dad. Doesn't she know this? Still, she yells. She yanked my ponytail. And I hate it all.

My eyes are watering again. I swipe them away. No way am I letting memories of Mom ruin my day here in Chicago.

Next I decide it's time to tackle all these notifications.

It appears Sierra was playing with phone filters in the middle of the night and sent me a cute photo of herself with raccoon ears. I giggle at the picture.

My friend Rachel from home wrote: Hope you're having a great time! Saw your tweet. TJ is cute!

There are a bunch of similar texts from other friends: You and TJ are cute together! Please tell me you got with him.

Next is a picture Austin sent to a big group of us. It's of him holding up a white flag with a smile on his face. The caption says: Won again! That's 18–11, losers!

I send back a "thumbs up" emoji.

The last message I click on is from T.J.:

Are we still on? I'm excited to see you.

I text T.J. back:

Yes. Can't wait.

A smile spreads across my face, happy that he seems like a good guy—straightforward and respectful and mature. And not to mention super sexy. The memory of him dancing close against my body... I won't be forgetting that anytime soon. I suddenly need to fan myself.

He seems really eager to hang out with me today. And he was so excited when we found each other again last night... I hope he's not more into me than I'm into him. I'd hate to hurt another guy. But he must know this is a weekend fling, right? We were clear with each other up front that I'm from Tennessee and that he lives in Wisconsin.

In the shower, I spend extra time lathering up my hair and shaving my legs—even the tough-to-get places around my knees and around my ankles. After I've dried off, I put on cutoffs and a halter top over my favorite pink bikini.

When I'm all ready to go, I quietly open the guest room door and peek out into the hallway. After making sure no one's in the hall, I tiptoe across a flowered rug that beautifully covers the hardwood floors leading to the kitchen. A vase full of colorful fake flowers sits on a glass side table across from an ivory and gray tile mosaic. Mom and I don't have anything like this in our duplex in Tennessee. Dad pays child support, of course, but it goes toward food and clothes, not decor.

My stepmother is an executive at a company that runs concessions stands at major sports venues around the country. I don't know for sure, but I bet Leah makes a ton of money. The one time I went to a Nashville Predators game, I paid fourteen bucks for a watered-down Coke and fries. Those soggy fries are probably how she and Dad can afford this Gold Coast apartment. I doubt they could on Dad's IT guy salary.

On top of having the best real estate, Leah has good taste and knows how to make a house look gorgeous. Sierra told me her mom loves going to flea markets and antique stores to find unique pieces on a dime.

If our house had looked more like this, would Dad have stayed?

The warm scent of coffee wafts through the air. Somebody's awake. That sucks. I'd hoped to sneak out of here before having to socialize.

"Good morning, Ladybug," a voice says. Dad is already awake, drinking coffee, and working on his laptop at the kitchen island, with no cares in the world. "Any interest in going for a walk down by the lake? Or to get brunch before y'all head back to the concert?"

Y'all. He still talks like he's from Tennessee, which hurts a little. Yet so much about him has changed.

Like, why is he wearing a button-down shirt at eight a.m. on a Saturday in July? This is a time for the grungiest, most comfortable T-shirts and shorts you own, not to get all dressed up like you have an important work meeting.

Since I arrived, he hasn't even bothered to ask how Mom is doing, or if I'm happy, or if I'm even okay. He didn't even take off work to pick me up at the airport. Sierra met me at O'Hare and we rode the train into the city.

And now he wants to spend time with me?

"I'm sorry," I reply. "I have plans."

Dad's face falls, but he covers it by taking a sip from his mug. And now I feel bad, because even though he hurt me more than I ever thought imaginable, I still love him. He's still my dad.

Plus, I need to be nice, because I need to talk to him about possibly moving here for college next year. "Can we go to breakfast tomorrow morning instead?"

He nods. "Of course. But where are you off to now?"

I straighten my bag looped over my shoulder. "Uh, breakfast and the beach."

"With Sierra? I hate to break it to you, but she won't be awake for"—he checks his watch—"another three hours."

"No, I'm going with this guy I know, T.J."

He narrows his eyes. "Who's T.J.?"

I decide to be honest. "A boy I met at the concert."

Dad shuts the lid on his laptop. "I don't think it's a good idea to go. And definitely not alone."

"Dad, trust me, it's fine. T.J.'s a nice guy."

"How do you know?"

Dad has a good point. I don't know T.J. at all. But I know myself, and I felt comfortable with him, like I'd known him for a long time. That sounds melodramatic—and not scientific in the least, but it's the truth.

And who is Dad to talk? He met his wife on the internet, the land where people misrepresent themselves. At least I met T.J. in person and am pretty sure he is who he says he is.

As long as we're in public in sight of other people, it should be safe to meet up with him.

"You're not going out with a boy you met yesterday," Dad says.

"I can tell he's normal," I snap back. "Besides, you should

know how it is. You're the one who met someone on the internet and ran off to meet her."

Dad cringes at my tone, then huffs defensively. "He could be an axe murderer for all we know."

An image of T.J.'s nervous, sweet smile comes to mind. "He's a teddy bear, if anything. Look, we want time to get to know each other better."

"I'm sure he does," Dad says in this deprecating tone. "Boys only want one thing."

"Ack!" I cringe. "God, Dad, shut up."

Dad sips his coffee. "Well, it's true."

It's not. T.J. asked me if I was okay last night before he slipped his hands around my waist. The memory makes my heart pound faster. He never would've forced me to do anything. Still, though, he's very good looking. With that body, he must do it all the time. Girls must be lining up to fall into his bed—he probably has a ticker tape machine like Skip's Deli back home.

And it's not like the thought didn't cross my mind. I want to hook up with him. Still, hearing your father talk about sex is worse than having a tooth pulled.

"I don't think it's fair of you to lump all guys together like that," I say. "I can tell T.J. is a good guy."

Dad shakes his head. "You're still not going alone. When you're staying with me, you listen to what I say."

Anger bubbles up inside me. He pays no attention to me most of the time—hasn't even asked how I'm doing, but he's directing me how to live my life?

I lash out, "I'm only staying for one more night." And with that, I adjust my bag on my shoulder and before Dad can even stand up from the barstool he's sitting on, I jog down the hall.

As I reach the front door, Leah comes in all sweaty, wearing leggings and a tank top. "Oh, hi, Mari. I'm just getting back from my run." She looks herself up and down. "Let me clean up and I'll come visit with you and your dad."

"Gotta jet!"

Leah opens her mouth to speak as I hurry out the front door.

I rush to the elevator and jab the lobby button several times. As I'm riding down eleven floors to the ground floor, a text lights up my phone.

Dad: Come back now.

I click the screen off and stow the phone in my bag. The elevator doors open, and I jog through the lobby.

A doorman talking on the phone holds up a hand and calls out to me, "Miss! Your father would like to speak with you—"

I ignore him and slip into the revolving door, which deposits me outside on the sidewalk. I take a left and hurry up the street toward the lake. Great. I'm on the lam.

T.J.

My body is running on pure adrenaline.

We didn't get back to Tyler's apartment until one in the morning. Then he stayed up late playing video games and drinking with Mike, who's also his roommate. As I tried to crash on the couch, the guys talked loudly and told every dirty joke known to man. I haven't laughed so hard in my entire life. But today I'm exhausted.

Normally I don't mind staying up late, but since I'm planning to meet Mari at ten for breakfast, I needed some rest.

And now I need coffee. While I'm waiting for it to brew, I text Mari to tell her I'm excited about today. Given that we're both leaving tomorrow, I decide to be direct and tell her what I'm feeling. I don't want to lose my chance with this girl. Whatever that chance might include.

I flick through my other notifications. So. Many. Notifications. The entire Twitter population must've been following whether Mari and I would find each other again last night. I switch over to Instagram and begin double-tapping the screen to like my friends' pictures. That's when I see I have a message request from Sierra Lavigne. I open it up.

Sierra: TJ! Here are some helpful tips! 1) Mari loves tulips, science, riding her bike, and snacks. Snacks are KEY. 2) She hates gross smells, so make sure you always smell great! 3) Do NOT avoid her texts. She hates that.

Science? That's intimidating. Of all the classes I took in school, I always had to study hardest for chemistry and physics. I start daydreaming of Mari tutoring me after school, her cute glasses perched on the tip of her nose, and she scolds me that I've been a *very bad student* and one thing leads to another and suddenly she's *tutoring* me in another type of science: biology. Sexy biology.

I jerk my head back and forth, to get my brain out of the gutter.

I read through Sierra's list again. *Bikes, tulips, candy.* Make sure I don't smell bad. Answer the phone. Basically, don't act like a caveman. Got it.

I'm glad to know more about Mari, but shouldn't I be learning about her naturally—from her? Sierra's little spy game seems wrong.

I push the button to begin following Sierra on Instagram, but decide not to respond to her "helpful tips." I don't want to encourage her. I'll get to know Mari the natural way.

The smell of coffee begins to waft through the room, but

it's still not finished brewing, so I sit back down on the couch and gaze around. Tyler's place is small with lots of sunlight. The kitchen opens directly into the living room, where he keeps the entertainment center and a few bookshelves full of knickknacks, photos, and his favorite things, like the baseball signed by the 2016 Cubs World Series team. His college diploma is hanging on the wall. In four years, will I be living in a place like this, with my University of Chicago diploma prominently on display?

Like Tyler, I declared business as my major. I haven't declared a minor yet because deep down inside, I want to pick media arts and design, and my family won't approve. According to Mom, Dad, and Tyler, math would make me more marketable when I'm searching for a job one day. The job market is tough, and I need every advantage I can get.

But I'm not even sure I want a job where I wear a suit every day. But that's what Mom and Dad do. Tyler too. It's what I'm supposed to do.

I have a sudden urge to paint a robot wearing a suit and tie, engulfed in flames.

The coffee maker beeps, telling me it's done. I'm nosing around in cabinets looking for a mug when a woman I've never seen before walks into the kitchen, wearing a long T-shirt that falls mid-thigh. When she sees me, she startles, bringing a hand to her chest.

Is she wearing any shorts? My eyes widen and my face begins to heat up in embarrassment. I quickly look away.

"Could I have some water?" she asks.

I find a glass in the cupboard for her, keeping my eyes lowered.

"Are you Tyler's brother?" she asks.

I nod. "I'm T.J. Are you here with Mike?" I scan my memories to remember his girlfriend's name. "Ashley?"

She shakes her head. "I'm Krysti. I came over to see Tyler."

"Oh." He hasn't mentioned her, but I don't say that.

Lowering her eyes, she brushes her hair behind an ear. "We met a few weeks ago."

She must have come over very late at night—after I fell asleep. How did Tyler convince her to come over at, like, three o'clock? That's late. It seems like the gentlemanly thing to do would've been to go to her place. But what do I know? Dad taught me the importance of holding doors open for ladies, but he never brought up booty call etiquette.

Is this what college will be like? Sometimes I forget I'm eighteen and don't have a curfew anymore. At eighteen, I'm already an adult, and adults do things like sleep over. I, me, T.J., can invite a girl to spend the night.

I mean, not at my house where my parents live—that would literally get me murdered by the aforementioned parents—but I could ask a girl over to my dorm in college.

It surprises me that Tyler would have a woman over when I'm staying here. Maybe he's finally starting to see me as more of a friend and not just his little brother.

Using the glass I handed her, Krysti pours herself some water from the Brita filter.

"You can have some coffee, too, if you want," I say.

"Oh, thank you," she replies, pushing a lock of hair behind her ear. "That would be great."

As I'm pouring us each a cup, she asks, "What are you doing today? Heading back to Lollapalooza?"

I stir milk into my coffee. "Yeah, tonight. First I'm going to breakfast and the beach with this girl I met yesterday."

Krysti raises her eyebrows as she sips from her mug. A door opens down the hallway, and Tyler emerges in a pair of basketball shorts and no shirt. At the sight of my brother, Krysti stands up straighter and begins mussing her hair.

Tyler yawns, then looks up to find me standing with Krysti. Suddenly his eyes open as if we startled him awake.

"Hey, what's going on?" he asks.

"T.J. made coffee," Krysti says, nudging my brother with a laugh. "You should try it sometime."

He laughs, but it sounds forced and nervous. He scrubs a hand through his hair. "You still going out with Mari today, T.J.?"

"Yeah," I say.

"If you want, you should come by my boat later," Krysti offers. "Well, it's my parents' boat. But I'm using it today. And you can come, too," she says to Tyler with a hopeful look on her face.

He gives a little shrug as he pulls another mug out of the cabinet. "I'm planning to go back to the concert."

When he says nothing else about making plans for today, she goes off down the hall shaking her head.

Once she's out of earshot, I ask, "Are you going out with her?"

He scratches the tip of his nose. "Not exactly... That's what she wants... But that's not what I'm looking for right now. But damn, she has a boat." He cocks his head. "Hmm."

Tyler pours himself a cup of coffee and drinks. He sticks out his tongue. "Man, T.J. Your coffee is absolute shit."

I laugh. "I've gotta get going to meet Mari."

With a grimace, Tyler takes another sip of coffee, then sets it on the counter. "Wait, let me get you some more condoms."

"No," I blurt. "I mean, I didn't even use the ones you gave me yesterday."

"Why not?"

Is he kidding me? When would we possibly have had time to do it? And where? "There was that whole we-got-separated thing? Also, we just met, you know."

"I know," he says with a shrug. "But you like her. You should go for it."

I don't understand how it's so easy for Tyler. How he can just do it like it's no big deal, and with a person he barely knows?

I guess it's different for everybody. The only thing I know is that while, yes, I want to have sex (obviously), I also want to get to know Mari better.

I don't know if I'd want to do the booty call thing. I want more than that. I want someone to talk to and spend time with.

Tyler takes a carton of eggs out of the fridge. "Want some food before you go?"

I'm tempted, because he's a great cook. All I can make is

a lazy-ass grilled cheese. I'm too lazy to make them the right way—in a frying pan with butter, so I toast two pieces of bread, then slip a slice of cheese between them and microwave it for thirty seconds. Voilà. A lazy-ass grilled cheese.

Right now Tyler is using the same hand to perfectly break three eggs at once. He lets them drip into a bowl. If I tried that, I'm sure I'd drop little pieces of shell into the pan.

If I want to keep eating well for my strength training at the gym, I need to learn how to do this sort of stuff before college. Mom won't be there to cook breakfast for me every day like she does now.

I'm starving, but I need to leave if I'm going to make it on time. "I'm out—I'm meeting Mari in half an hour."

He fist-bumps me and gives me a big grin. "Good luck, man."

I gulp the rest of my coffee, throw my beach towel over a shoulder, and head out. I'm all smiles as I jog down three flights of stairs to the lobby and out to the street, which is surprisingly empty. No cars, a few pedestrians. My brother's apartment is on the South Side near where he went to school at the University of Chicago. Kids probably haven't come back from summer break yet.

I catch a Ryde up to the Gold Coast area, where Mari said her dad lives, to meet her at a cafe near Washington Square Park. It's close enough to the beach to walk there after breakfast.

On the drive, I check various apps on my phone. IG, ESPN, Twitter. In my feed, I see that If We Were Giants retweeted a post from a Chicago radio station:

Want to go backstage at #Lollapalooza and meet If We Were Giants? Play WTGP Radio's LollaScavengerHunt! Two lucky winners will go backstage on Sunday. Follow WTGP for prompts throughout the day. Details here!

Shit! It would be amazing to meet those guys. Not only do I love their music, I love the cover art on their albums. Their bass player, Adam Tracy, designs them. It's something they're known for. I'd love to talk to him about his art and how it fits into his life. Clearly it's not his number one job, but he manages to do what he loves all the same.

I click on the Twitter link to read more about the contest. The radio station will be tweeting Chicago landmarks throughout today. People are supposed to go around Chicago, find the landmarks, and take selfies to prove they were there. For a chance to win, you have to find all the landmarks. Creativity is encouraged.

With a click of my thumb, I follow the radio station's Twitter account and set my account to notify me when there's a new post. I doubt I'll have time to take all the selfies, but I can at least try.

For the rest of the Ryde trip, I call up my sketchpad app and pull my stylus pen out of my pocket. Tyler said he wanted a hula girl tattoo? I begin to sketch a hula girl. She has a green grass skirt on, but I give her purple spiky hair, a nose ring, and a cute pair of glasses like Mari's. I add tiny pink tulips to the ends of her grass skirt.

I smile at the drawing. Then I feel that itch. That pull. The deep one inside me, luring me to spray paint this punk hula girl on the concrete underpass next to my green alien.

I dream of it until my Ryde pulls up in front of the Newberry Library by Washington Square Park. I love this part of the city. It's so green and there's a lot to do here.

As I climb out of the car, I use my phone to give the driver a tip and rate him five stars. For the safe ride, but also for karmic purposes. When I look up from my screen, Mari's waiting outside under the cafe's awning, kneading her fingers together.

She hasn't noticed me yet and it's creepy I'm standing here watching her, but I don't know if I should hug her, or maybe side-hug her? Kiss her cheek? Give her a wave?

Why didn't I ask Tyler what to do? Not that it would've mattered. He'd have just said something like, "Do what feels right in your gut."

My gut doesn't know shit.

"T.J."

I snap out of it to find Mari hurrying my way with a tote bag bouncing against her side. When she reaches me, both of us suddenly stop. At night, I didn't hesitate to pull her into my arms. Out here under the sun, she can probably see the hesitation all over my face.

Before I can make a decision, she gets up on tiptoes and wraps her arms around my neck. "Good morning."

I return the hug. "Good morning," I murmur into her dark, curly hair. It smells so good. This feels unreal, like I'm starring in a movie about a much luckier guy's life.

With a smile, she asks, "Hungry?"

My mouth waters at the smells of bacon and sausage. "Let's go."

Mari leads me inside, where a host seats us in a booth with retro leather benches the color of red M&Ms. Warm morning light beams through the window.

Mari adjusts her glasses to read the menu. "I've never been here, but Sierra says it's good. She said we should order the french toast."

"Sure, but we're getting bacon and eggs too. And an english muffin."

"That's a lot."

"I eat a ton," I admit. "It helps me in the gym."

After we order, the server brings us steaming hot mugs of coffee.

Mari stirs in cream along with several fake sugars, while I pour milk into mine. I stop pouring when it changes from black to my preferred murky brown color.

She sips from her mug, crinkles her nose, and dumps in another fake sugar. When she tests it this time, she smiles, apparently satisfied with her mix. She's beyond cute. How will I make it through breakfast without leaning across the table to kiss her?

As casually as I can, I adjust my shorts, trying to hide that I'm turned on. I doubt anybody's checking out my junk under the table, but you never know. There could be creepy junk-checker-out-ers around.

Mari keeps one hand on her mug and uses the other to push her hair behind her ear. "So we didn't get to talk much last night."

"Kind of hard when you lose each other for two hours."

She laughs. "It was good luck that Sierra secretly took a picture of us."

"I know. Normally I have bad luck when it comes to girls."

"You? Really?"

My face burns. Not sure why I blurted that out. "Yes, really. I honestly can't believe I'm on a date right now... This is a date, right?"

She raises her eyebrows as her cheeks turn pink. "When was your last date?"

I scratch behind my ear, wondering if I should make something up. But I like Mari so much, I want to be real with her.

I decide to tell her the truth. "It's embarrassing."

Mari

It can't be that embarrassing.

"Tell me about the date," I say.

T.J. crosses his arms on the table, then reaches up to scratch his head. "My best friend Ethan was planning to go to senior prom with his girlfriend, Reese. He had everything planned. A limo, dinner, a hotel room."

"Okay," I say, wondering what this has to do with his last date.

"But at the last minute, Ethan got the chicken pox."

"The chicken pox? For real?"

T.J. shrugs. "He never had it as a kid, and his parents didn't get him the vaccine, which wasn't smart. Anyway, he didn't want to let Reese down—she had this dress she wanted to wear, so he begged me to go in his place. Reese and I took Ethan's limo and used his dinner reservation, but uh, not the hotel room obviously." T.J. coughs into his fist. "I didn't even have a tux, and it was too late to rent one. I had to borrow a suit from Tyler."

"It's a good thing you're close to his same size."

T.J. grins at that. "I wasn't always his size. I used to be a lot skinnier. I've been working out a lot this year."

I try to picture him smaller. Did he look like Steve Rogers before his transformation into Captain America? I scan T.J.'s chest, swallowing hard. Most guys I know wear slouchy tees with baggy sweatpants. He fills out his gray T-shirt just right. It makes me want to know what's under that T-shirt.

Is it hot in here?

Our server appears next to the table, balancing plates of french toast, eggs, bacon, and fruit. She slides the food in front of us and tops off our coffees.

Steam wafts up from my mug. After pouring syrup on my french toast, I pick up my fork to dig in. "So you didn't have a date to prom already?"

He shakes his head. "I wasn't planning to go. There wasn't anyone I wanted to ask." His eyes meet mine. "Too bad I hadn't met you."

I take a deep breath. This boy is dangerous.

I glance up at T.J. He's still watching me closely. It should make me uncomfortable, but I feel safe with him, like it's okay to be real.

"I haven't dated much," I admit, which is mostly true. I haven't had an official boyfriend, but I did make out with Austin, and before him, I'd kissed two guys when I was younger. I've never been on a date before.

T.J. pauses with a forkful of eggs on the way to his mouth.

Then he nods, before finishing the bite. He stares out the window as he continues to dig into his food.

I'm not sure what to say next.

He was honest with me about how his prom date situation embarrassed him, so I wanted to be open as well. But now I'm worried I've scared him off by basically admitting I'm a virgin.

What if he's looking for a weekend fling with a girl who has experience?

"That doesn't bother you, right? That I haven't dated much?" I ask quietly.

He shakes his head. "Not at all. I'm just surprised. You're so confident and nice and beautiful..." He suddenly crams a big bite of french toast in his mouth and chews. "I haven't really dated either."

I laugh nervously. "That's not what I figured."

He smirks a little. "Why? What did you think? That I'm some sort of lothario?"

"Yup, that's exactly what I thought. That you're a sex fiend."

"C'mon. For real, what did you think?"

"Just that—" I take a deep breath. "That you must have lots of experience. I mean, the way you were dancing with me last night... It was like you know what you're doing. Like, reeeeally know what you're doing."

His eyes lock on me. "That's all because of you."

While T.J. uses the bathroom before we head to the beach, I check my phone to find messages from Mom and Dad, both telling me to go home to Dad's apartment *RIGHT NOW*.

Shit. Dad dragged Mom into this?

I ignore the texts, then try to ignore my guilt. I don't want to worry Mom or piss her off—she's already angry enough I came to Chicago. I shiver when I think of how she yanked on my ponytail. How she yelled at me. I don't want that to happen again.

And I'm pissed at Dad too. How dare he suddenly start acting like a parent, telling me I'm not allowed to date?

I'm not giving up this time with T.J.

I've never lacked for friends, and if I go to a party or school dance, there's always someone to talk to. But everyone's usually interested in someone hooking up with or dating someone else.

I've never experienced this: a guy I'm into, who's wholly into me, and I can definitely fool around with him if we both want to.

A text from Sierra pops up:

Sierra: David's pissed.

Me: Can you get Dad to call off the attack?

Sierra: No. He's really upset with you. I'm surprised he hasn't called the cops.

Me: Ughhhh. Why does he care?

Sierra: He's your dad. Obvs. I told him TJ is nice and to leave you alone... I don't think it worked.

Me: I love you anyway.

Sierra: I love you toooooo! I'll try to get David to back off so you can boink TJ

Me: BOINK?!

Sierra: Boink!

Has my stepsister lost her mind?

A text from Leah pops up next: Your dad and I are looking forward to spending time with you this weekend. Let me know when?

Her message makes me feel even guiltier. But not guilty enough to go back to my dad's place.

The bathroom door swings open, and T.J. comes out. He looks over at me, stops walking, and smiles. His blue eyes focus on me for so long, it's like he forgets to move. A server rushes by, jostling him out of his trance.

He approaches the table and gently touches my shoulder. "Everything okay?"

"My dad wanted to spend time with me today."

His eyebrows pinch together. "Do you need to go?"

I shake my head.

He pulls his sunglasses down over his eyes. "You ready to hit the beach?"

The sun beats down on us as we walk toward the lake. To get to the beach, we have to go down a set of concrete stairs and cross under Lake Shore Drive through a tunnel.

It's gross in here. Lots of mud puddles full of trash and floating discarded plastic bottles. I want to get through here as quickly as possible without getting my feet dirty. I hold my breath so I don't have to smell any gross smells.

T.J., however, flips his sunglasses up on top of his head and stops to look at a graffiti mural on the concrete wall. It's a portrait of Obama wearing a Chicago Cubs uniform.

"Oh, that's cool," T.J. says. He pulls out his phone and snaps a couple pictures of the mural, as well as some of the other graffiti down here. I've never seen anyone do that before. But what really captures his attention is a beam of sunlight shining through a grate onto a bare section of concrete, surprisingly untouched by graffiti. He looks back and forth from the sunbeam to the wall, then steps up and touches it, like it's a blank canvas.

Is T.J. a graffiti artist? I want to ask, but that seems deeply personal, not to mention illegal. Even if I ask, he may not feel comfortable telling me if he's into it.

As soon as we climb the steps on the other side, I let out the breath I was holding. The smell didn't seem to bother T.J. Maybe he's used to hanging out in gross tunnels, doing graffiti.

Alongside the beach is an asphalt pathway. It's nearly as busy as the highway we just crossed under, crowded with people walking their dogs and exercising, running, and Rollerblading. T.J. puts an arm out in front of me, stopping me from nearly walking out in front of cyclists. I give him a grateful nod, glad not to end up roadkill.

Once we're across, we walk closer to the shore. Every time I see Lake Michigan, I mistake it for the Atlantic Ocean, so vast and azure blue. A hundred feet away, a bunch of boats are clustered offshore. Sunbathers lie on yacht decks, listening to loud rap music. The bass thumps along with my heart.

If I look up and to my right, skyscrapers fill the blue sky. Right here, at high tide, the water rushes over the walkways onto the bike path, slowly erasing a pink chalk drawing of a house.

T.J. points down the shoreline. "Want to sit on the beach?" Some people are sitting on the concrete next to the shore, but I'd prefer the sand. With his hand in mine, I pull him in that direction.

It's not even noon yet, but the beach is packed with people lounging under umbrellas, pulling cold drinks out of coolers. A plane pulling an advertisement for beer flies overhead.

T.J. and I spread out our towels on the sand a few feet away from other people.

With a deep breath, I pull my halter top off over my head and unbutton my jean shorts, slowly pushing them down to reveal my pink bikini. I worry what he thinks of my body. He's so strong and fit, and while I'm trim, I still feel flabby in certain places.

I make a midyear resolution to immediately start doing more crunches. Is now a good time to start? Right here on the beach?

Another plane flies overhead. This one's pulling an ad for Trojan condoms.

My face feels like it's on fire. I swear. Is the universe out to embarrass me?

Keeping my head tilted down, I sneak a peek at T.J. Even though he's wearing sunglasses, I can tell he's checking me out. Our gazes meet, and he swallows hard.

I pull sunscreen out of my bag, sit down, and begin lathering up my arms and legs, making sure not to miss anywhere.

"Do you need help with your back?" he asks.

I hand him my bottle. "Yeah, I burn bad sometimes."

He gives me a smile as he begins to work the lotion into my shoulder. His strong hands knead my skin, and I say a little prayer that there will be a chance for him to give me a full-body massage, because *wow*. When he starts on my back, I bite my bottom lip, to stop myself from groaning.

Once he's given me two solid coats of sunscreen—*I bet he'd continue slathering it on all day, if I let him*—I lie on my towel. T.J. pulls his T-shirt off over his head, revealing his tanned body. His chest is strong, and a thin strip of hair points down from his belly button to below his swimsuit. My mouth waters at the muscular V-shape of his waist.

I watch him out of the corner of my eye. "I'd ask if you want me to put sunscreen on your back, but you clearly don't need it."

He grins and playfully says, "Sure, I do. Everybody needs sunscreen."

"Are you just saying that so I'll touch you?"

"Maybe." He lies down, turning on his side to face me. He reaches out to intertwine our fingers together. With my other hand I touch his forearm, unable to keep my hands to myself.

He looks at where I'm touching him and starts laughing. "Last night, before I found you, I thought my brother was going to go make us get hula girl tattoos on our forearms."

I laugh. "That sounds awful. I mean, can you get a job if you have a tattoo like that? You'd have to make sure it's covered all the time. Then what's the point?"

"Right? If you're going to get a tattoo, you should show it off. Have it on display like a piece at a museum."

I've never heard anyone describe a tattoo that way.

"Do you want a tattoo?" he asks.

Tattoos are not my thing. "If I were to get one, I guess I'd have to get...a taco."

He grins. "A taco?"

"I think that's the only thing I love enough."

"You're cute."

"What would you get?" I ask him.

He tilts his head, then swipes on his phone screen. He taps it a bunch of times and turns the screen around so I can see. "This is the plan. Do you like it?"

I peer at the screen. It's difficult to see in the sun, but slowly my eyes come into focus.

At first glance, it looks like a bunch of black, red, and green symbols—some appear raised, some sunken, but as my eyes zero in, I discover its chain links that swirl like a tail into the body of a dragon. Instead of blowing orange sparks, the dragon is spitting blue fire. If I let my eyes wander, it becomes a bunch of shapes again. An elaborate optical illusion.

"That's so cool. I love it."

He nods, and looks up at me, and smiles.

"You're really gonna get that?" I ask. "Where?"

T.J. points below his hip and drags his finger up his side. I imagine the chain winding along his hip bone and lateral muscles. I've never been into the idea of tattoos, but right now? His plan sounds hot. Very hot.

As we stare at each other, his hand gently sweeps up my wrist along my arm to my elbow, then back down again. This time his hand stops on my waist, his fingertips gently drumming my skin. He plays with the string on my bikini bottoms, boldly twisting it between his fingers. A confident move, but his hand is shaking.

I'm shaking too.

T.J.

My fingers can't stop touching the smooth skin of her hip.

I want to press my mouth to it.

I want to press my mouth everywhere.

She leans in toward me, closing her eyes, coming halfway. I shut my eyes too.

I can do this. I can kiss her. She's not going to turn me down.

Is she?

What if we kiss and she pulls away? What if, after kissing me once, she doesn't want more? That's what happened with Lacey. What if nothing's wrong with me, but something's wrong with my kissing? Shit.

It's not as if I really know how to kiss anyway. I'm likely bad at it just because I've barely done it. Maybe if I had more practice...

Maybe my brother's right. Tyler said to find a girl who sets me on fire, and then I'd know what to do.

So I do it.

I take off my sunglasses, lean forward, and go the rest of the way.

Her lips are soft. So soft I groan. I hold my breath, expecting her to yank away from me. But she doesn't. She opens her mouth, inviting me in.

I'm so excited I want to climb to the top of a mountain, raise my fists, and scream to the world, "We're fucking kissing!"

Her glasses press against my cheek uncomfortably. I break the kiss momentarily, to help her take them off. "These are so cute," I tell Mari as I set them carefully on top of her bag. "But they're in our way."

She gives me a tiny, shy grin.

Once her glasses are gone, I run a hand through her curly hair, pulling Mari closer. Our eyes meet before I gently roll her onto her back and press my mouth to hers. The feel of her chest against mine drives me wild. Makes me kiss her harder.

"Get a room!" some guy calls out.

Suddenly she stops kissing me and pulls to the side, breathing heavily, her eyes shut. "Wait."

I pull my hand from where my fingers had been tangled in her bikini bottoms string. "You okay?"

Mari bites her lower lip, clearly not okay.

I want to touch her arm, but I don't want to freak her out either. Instead I pick up some sand and let it sift through my fingers, to do something with my hand so I won't go back to touching her. "I'm sorry. Did I move too fast?"

"A little. I mean, we're in public." She giggles nervously. "Pretty soon we were gonna be in R-rated territory."

"We were?" I blurt out like a high soprano, and I'm so embarrassed I want to throw myself in the lake.

"And I barely know you," she says. "I don't normally move so fast."

I roll over onto my back and peer up at the sky. The bright sun hurts my eyes. I'm glad. Maybe burning the shit out of my retinas will give me something to concentrate on besides how I'm blowing it with another girl.

Her fingers circle my wrist. "But I want to know more about you."

She does?

Relief spreads through my whole body, reminding me of the time Ethan and I broke into his dad's liquor stash. Mari wanting to know more about me is a smooth shot of whiskey to my heart.

I stare at her. "What do you want to know?"

"I dunno... Tell me two truths and a lie."

"Okay, let's see." I take a few seconds to think. "I ran cross-country for my high school, I love watching horror movies, and I am terrible at cooking."

She rolls over onto her elbow to face me. "Is it the cross-country running?"

I shake my head. "Horror movies freak me out. I went to see this one horror movie with Ethan. It was about how if you got a text from this unknown number with this meme of a ghoul, you only had seven days to live. The people who died? Their faces, like, melted off. Like, gooey cheese pizza."

Mari rolls her eyes.

"Hey! I was scared as shit. I left the movie, went out to the lobby, and played video games. And I was still freaked out, even though it was broad daylight outside. After that movie, I couldn't check my texts for a whole day."

We laugh together.

Mari's phone beeps. She lifts it to check the screen. Her eyes balloon. Her lower lip begins to quiver. "I just got a text. It's...it's...a ghoul."

"Shit, what?" I grab the phone from her hand as she cracks up.

"Just kidding. It was another message from Dad. Not the murderous ghoul."

I work to catch my breath. "That was not funny." What if it was like the movie and she died in seven days?

Mari curls her elbow under her head and uses it as a pillow, her hair spilling down her arm. "Do you forgive me?"

I give her a playful evil eye. "We'll see. First you have to give me two truths and a lie."

"Okay, hmmm." She licks her lips and pushes a lock of hair behind her ear. "My favorite TV show is *Dancing with the Stars*, I'm president of my school's STEM club, and I love camping."

I'm glad Sierra gave me the heads-up that Mari's into science. I know it's not STEM. I squint at her as I think. "*Dancing with the Stars*?"

"No! I love that show. It's the camping." She shudders. "I

hate bugs and snakes and anything with creepy-crawly legs. I hate being dirty."

"And you came to Lollapalooza?" I say in a deadpan voice, which makes her laugh. "It's gonna take me ten more showers to get off the grime from last night."

"I know! My Converse are ruined." She points over at the silver sneakers she slipped off when we arrived at the beach. They're all muddy and stained. "I don't even want to know what I stepped in."

I smile at her. "So. STEM club? As if you weren't already intimidating."

She looks pleased at that. A smile stretches across her face as she intertwines her fingers with mine. Mari rolls a little closer to me, like before, and I want to fire a T-shirt gun into the crowd to celebrate that I didn't totally screw up with her.

"Let's play again," she says. "Tell me two truths and a lie. Serious ones this time."

She truly does want to get to know me, and I want to know her too. But we live so far apart, it's hard to imagine anything happening between us beyond this weekend. Do I want to tell Mari secrets about me, to get to know her even better, knowing I'll have to leave her?

Mari licks her lips, looking expectant, her brown eyes boring into mine. And I'm lost.

"I'm scared I'll never be as great at anything as my brother—sometimes I feel like I'm an inferior copy of him. My favorite football team is the Chicago Bears...and I'm a virgin."

She stares at me. A red flush appears on her neck and chest.

"You're from Wisconsin, so I'm guessing you love the Green Bay Packers. Is the Bears the lie?"

"God, yes, I hate the Bears."

Mari touches a hand to her throat. "Your truth—the last one. It's, um, surprising."

I can't believe I told her. "I wanted you to know I don't go fast either. I didn't mean to freak you out before. I got...carried away."

She lowers her eyes. "I'm also surprised you told me."

"I wanted to be up front, I guess. I didn't know what you'd expect from me..."

"What'd you think I would expect? Breakfast and then immediate sex?"

I laugh nervously.

She tilts her head as if thinking. "I do expect some sort of pastry. Maybe a strawberry-jam-filled donut."

Sierra was right. I should have snacks handy. "That can be arranged."

Her eyes fall to my lips. And then she's kissing me again.

Mari

I'm lying on the beach kissing a boy.

I'm kissing a boy, and I'm loving it. The kiss tastes rich and addictive. T.J. can't keep his hands off me. He nuzzles his face in my neck, leaving gentle but steamy kisses on my skin.

But as we fall more and more into each other, his interest in me begins to seem more real, beyond the physical, and not fleeting. I'm not entirely sure how I know this. I'm just sure it's true.

The kissing feels so good I don't want it to end, but maybe I should have a conversation with T.J. to lay some ground rules for what we're doing. Maybe that's unnecessary since I'm leaving tomorrow? Maybe I should just go with how good and right this feels.

Then my brain falls away, and I concentrate on the feel of his warm skin, the taste of his lips.

My phone buzzes on my lap. I pause from kissing T.J. to squint at the screen. It's difficult to see it out here under the sun.

I fumble for my glasses and put them back on. The screen blinks. *Mom calling. Mom calling.*

Oh no. She's moved beyond texts.

Now things are serious. If there's one thing Mom hates, it's talking on the phone. She must be losing her patience with me.

"I have to take this," I tell T.J. "It's Mom."

He lets out a deep breath—he's probably as worked up from kissing as I am—and gives me a happy smile as he relaxes back on his towel with an arm tucked behind his head.

Clenching my eyes shut, I swipe on to answer the phone.

"Mari, why haven't you been answering my messages?"

"Sorry, Mom. I was eating breakfast at a cafe and didn't want to be rude."

"Your father called me. Said you ran off with a boy?"

I can tell she's trying to keep her voice measured, but she's also annoyed. I'm annoyed with her. She didn't bother to text me until she found out I'm with T.J. Rude.

"I didn't run off," I tell her. "I told Dad where I was going."

"He didn't give you permission to go."

"He was being unreasonable."

"Running off with a boy you just met is what sounds unreasonable."

"It's not. I have good judgment, you know. And so does Sierra. She likes him."

Mom pauses. She doesn't like hearing about Sierra. It only reminds her she was unable to have another baby, and now Dad has a stepdaughter.

Mom huffs into the phone. "Who is this boy?"

"T.J. He's perfectly normal, I promise."

At my words, T.J. tenses up. He pulls himself up into a seated position and crosses his legs, scratching the side of his head. Even though we just met, I know he does that when he's nervous. He pushes his messy blond hair to the side and peeks up at me.

"I don't feel good about this," Mom says.

"I'm fine. We're on a public beach in the middle of downtown Chicago. Nothing's going to happen to me here. A hundred people would see if he tried to kidnap me."

"You never know what might happen."

"And that's why you had us take those self-defense lessons. I can defend myself. Anything goes wrong, I'll knee him in the balls like I did with Asshole Bob."

T.J. cringes and pulls his knees to his chest with a look of utter horror.

Mom tsks into the phone. "Your dad's angry and wants you to go back to his place. I need you to go. I don't like talking to him on the phone, and he's already called me twice this morning. How could you do this to me?"

Of course she'd make this all about her. Talking to Dad hurts her, so I shouldn't be able to do what I want. She can't even take two seconds to ask if I'm enjoying my trip, if I like T.J., or if I'm happy.

Dad didn't bother to ask if I'm happy either.

I'm nearly an adult. I can make my own decisions, especially when it comes to how I spend my time.

"Don't worry about me," I tell her. "I'll talk to you later."

"You bet we'll be talking later," Mom says in a mean voice. "We'll be talking about how you're grounded the beginning of your senior year. You can forget about homecoming and going to any football games. You can forget about the things you're looking forward to. Lord knows *I* have nothing to look forward to."

And then she hangs up on me.

Shit, shit, shit.

I pull my legs to my chest so I can bury my face in my knees. I hate it when she says things like that. *I have nothing left to look forward to.* She doesn't even try to get her life back. She just sits around and says things like this, to make everyone else around her feel bad and guilty.

Is Mom serious about grounding me? The best part of school is going to football games, especially now that I'm a senior and will be cheering in the stands with the spirit squad.

It's like, if she's not happy, no one else should be happy. Not even her daughter.

Why doesn't Mom care about my happiness as much as her own?

My mind keeps flowing back to whether I should ask Dad if I can move here for senior year. When Mom called, she was so angry with me. She would see me moving as a betrayal. She may never be happy again after that.

My life is a hot mess.

T.J. clears his throat. "Who's Asshole Bob? Your ex?"

I glance up. "No, he's the mannequin we beat up at self-defense class."

"Whew. I mean, I know Bob's an asshole, but I feel bad for anybody who gets whacked in the junk."

I bang my forehead against my knees. This sucks.

T.J. rests a hand on my forearm. "Is everything all right? Do you need to go?"

"Same ol', same ol'. My parents are being stupid."

"Your parents are divorced?"

"Yeah. For a few years now."

"You want to talk about it?" he asks quietly.

It would be easier to talk if we were in the dark. I hate talking about my feelings in daylight, because my traitor face shows every personal thing in my heart. "It sucks... It feels like they care more about themselves than me. It's always about them."

T.J. intertwines his fingers with mine. "I'm sorry."

"Are your parents together?"

"Yeah. I'm pretty lucky, I think. I mean, they embarrassed the hell out of me on my eighteenth birthday. They sent this huge balloon arrangement to school, and it showed up during calculus. But I know they love me, you know?"

"My parents love me too. It's just, things are weird."

T.J.'s eyes are attentive, so I slowly begin to tell him a little about what happened with my parents, and how things are now. How I feel guilty even trying to live my life, because Mom is so unhappy.

"I see what you mean," he says. "It does sound like they're all about themselves. But you should be number one."

As he says it, I realize it's true. I wish I were somebody's number one.

The thought sends little butterflies fluttering through my body.

T.J.

As we lie here on the beach together, the conversation doesn't stop. It doesn't stall. It gets better and better as we move from the serious to fun topics and back again.

The questions keep flowing.

"Where's your favorite place you've been?" I ask Mari.

She rolls onto her stomach, using her arms as a pillow, and looks at me sideways. "I haven't traveled a whole lot. But there's this little town in Florida we went to one time. It's called Seaside. Every single house there looks like it's been redone by those *Fixer Upper* people on HGTV. They're all painted Easter colors."

I scrunch my nose, imagining all those cookie-cutter houses with their horrible ordinary pastels.

She smacks my arm. "Hey! It was pretty."

"I'm glad Easter's only once a year. I can't handle all those baby blues and soft pinks."

"Annnyway," she drawls, cutting me off. I smile at her boldness. "I loved Seaside. Everyone is so nice, and the town is clean. No one drives—everyone walks everywhere. There was a little market and a butcher shop. A little soap store, with homemade soaps and bath bombs and bubble bath..."

I fake a yawn.

"...an old record store."

"Okay, now you're talking."

She touches my arm. "You'd love Seaside, T.J."

It doesn't seem like my thing, but I'd spend all day in a soap store smell testing bath bombs if Mari was there. I'm surprised, though, that she seems into something so perfect. She seemingly wants everything in its place, which I get—some people are like that, and that's okay, but I didn't expect that of her. I thought she might be more impulsive. I mean, she agreed to hang out with the guy she just met in the Ryde.

"What did you mean before about your brother?" she asks. "Why do you think you're inferior to him?"

I turn onto my back and stare at the sky with my sunglasses on. I cross one leg over the other, trying to get comfortable.

"T.J.?"

I scrub my hand through my hair. It's a mess. "I dunno. He got nearly a perfect score on the math section of the SAT."

"Wow."

"And that same year, I barely made a B in algebra I."

"Okay, so some of us are better at certain subjects than others."

"Tyler and I were both on the track team. He won the mile and two mile all the time. I never came in higher than third place."

"So that's just sports and math. There must be something you're better at."

But what if sports and math are what your family care about? If you aren't good at the same things as your family—if you don't even care about those things, it's hard not to feel second rate.

Mari's looking at me expectantly. Gotta give her something.

"At graduation, I won Most Artistic," I say quietly. Her mouth forms an O, and her brown eyes go soft. "And for the yearbook superlatives, I was voted Most Artistic there too." I shrug. "My parents congratulated me on the awards, but they were more excited I graduated in the top ten percent."

"What'd your brother say?"

"He said, 'Huh, cool. Ready to go eat?' He was excited because my parents were taking us to this fancy steak place to celebrate my graduation."

With a smile, she shakes her head. Haven't even known her a day, but I think she understands Tyler's antics. "You must be really artistic."

"I mean, I was always the kid at summer camp who wanted to stay in the arts and crafts pavilion instead of going to the pool or to play field games. I love painting. And making stuff."

"Like what?"

I lift up my wrist and show her some of my leather and cloth bracelets.

She touches them with her fingers. "You made these? I figured you bought them."

Her pointer finger gently touches my favorite one, the leather braided cord with the single Swarovski crystal. When the sun hits it, it shines like a far-off star. It didn't take long to make, but it came out looking like something you can buy in a store.

"I love this one," she says.

Without letting myself think too much about it, I unclasp it, take her hand, and slip it over her wrist.

Mari

I run my fingers over the leather bracelet.

My pulse is pounding hard.

This is the first time a boy has given me a gift like this. Something personal from the heart. Is that what it means?

I tell myself it's only a bracelet.

It hangs a lot more loosely on my arm than his, so I push it up my forearm several inches.

He sits up, crosses his legs in front of him, and holds out his hands. "Let me see it. I'll fix it."

With deft fingers, he detaches the clasp. He reaches into his pocket, pulls out a set of keys, and flips through them to a small Swiss Army knife key chain. He quickly measures the bracelet on my arm, then uses the tiny knife to cut off a couple centimeters of leather. T.J. looks up into my eyes before reattaching the clasp. Once it's ready, he unhooks it and slips it back onto my wrist.

I hold up my arm to study it. It fits perfectly. "T.J.? Did you make the design for your tattoo?"

He fidgets with his key chain, closing up the knife and thrusting it back into his pocket. Finally, he nods.

"Why didn't you tell me? You're so talented."

He glances up at me. "Too personal, I guess."

Meeting T.J. is like peeling an onion. The more time I spend with him, I uncover more layers, more intricacies. I continue to notice more and more things I like about him. Like his long eyelashes. I enjoy peeking under them in search of his blue eyes.

"The way you're looking at me," T.J. says. "I really need to kiss you again."

I touch the bracelet. "Then why aren't you?"

Right as he reaches for me, my phone beeps. It's Sierra's ringtone, or I wouldn't bother to look.

Sierra: I'm coming to the beach. Where are you?

Me: On the sand at Oak St. Beach. You're here?

Sierra: On my way!

I look up at T.J. "Sierra's coming to meet us."

T.J. sighs, then stretches his arms over his head. He puts his sunglasses back on. Now that I've gotten to know him better, he's even more attractive.

"C'mere," I tell him, wrapping my hand around the back of his neck, pulling him close for a long kiss. As I become more comfortable with him, the kissing is even better than before. I'm drowning.

His hand gently cradles my face. "Mmm."

We break apart, breathing heavily.

"I had to do that before my sister gets here," I say. "I couldn't help it."

"Me neither."

Sierra and Megan arrive, both wearing cute bikini tops and jean shorts. My stepsister squeals. "I'm so glad you guys found each other. You're so perfect together!"

Megan plops her beach bag down on the sand and smiles at us. "So cute," she adds.

"What are you guys doing here?" I ask, half pleased, half annoyed. She knows T.J. and I aren't together, can never be together, yet she's acting like we're heading for the altar later today.

"I told David and Mom I was coming down here. It got them to back off on calling the Marines in to rescue you."

I laugh. "Thanks."

"You really owe us," Megan says, flipping her chic sunglasses down over her eyes. "Having to come outside in the sun and lie on the beach? We're sacrificing a lot."

Sierra smacks her arm. "You'd be here anyway, and you know it."

Megan smiles at Sierra, who tucks a piece of blond hair behind an ear. It's her nervous tic. Sierra's never mentioned she's interested in Megan, but I'd bet Vegas money she is.

Megan fans herself. "I'm burning up. Going to cool off. Be right back."

She takes off toward the water, her braids bouncing against her back. Sierra watches as Megan wades into the lake.

Right as I'm wondering what's going on with them, T.J. asks, "Is Megan your girlfriend?"

Sierra, who had been arranging her pink towel on the sand, pauses for a long moment, then goes back to straightening it. "No, she's one of my best friends. What gave you that idea?"

"Oh. Sorry about that," T.J. says.

Maybe Sierra doesn't know how she feels. To me, though, it's clear as today's blue sky. "T.J. has a point," I say carefully. "It seems like you're into her."

Sierra gives me a look of death, then pulls her sunglasses down over her eyes. "Even if I did like Megan, I can't go out with her. Megan's a friend." Sierra pushes her blond hair back, sweeping it into a ponytail. "If we got together, it could mess everything up."

"Who says it would get messed up?" I ask.

My stepsister faces the lake, where Megan has waded to where the water is up to her waist. "It's not a good idea to tell a friend you want more. I mean, look what happened to you and Austin."

I raise my eyebrows at her in warning.

"I'm sorry," Sierra says quickly. "I didn't mean to say that. It came out before I thought about what I was saying. I'm sorry, Mari."

She looks truly apologetic, so I give her a quick nod, showing I forgive her, that I will always forgive her.

I peek over at T.J. to find his forehead creased. He must be wondering what Sierra and I are talking about, but I don't want to tell him. Thinking about my best friend hurts.

But T.J. is worried, so I need to give him something. "It's in the past."

He lets out a breath he'd been holding. "Okay."

Sierra waves at us. "C'mon, I need another picture of you two. All of Twitter wants to know if you guys got together. Even Chrissy Teigen. Scoot closer together."

T.J. throws an arm around my shoulders. I cozy up next to him and lean my head against his shoulder.

"Smile!" Sierra taps her phone screen several times, snapping pictures of us. She posts one to her IG story and tags me. I swipe my phone on to look at the photo. T.J. and I look great together.

I navigate to my IG account and repost Sierra's picture to my story.

T.J. nudges my shoulder. "Can you send me that picture?"

I text it to him and watch as he posts it to his IG feed.

That's when Austin responds to my IG story: You look happy

Me: It's been a nice day

I think, *I like talking to T.J.*, but I don't tell Austin that. It's too personal. It's like a tiny seed buried deep inside me, a seed that could easily grow into a beautiful red tulip. But until you water it, a seed stays a seed. It needs to stay ungrown. Because once it grows, it will eventually wither away.

T.J. leans against my arm, peeking at me sideways. The light seems to have gone out of his face. What is he thinking?

And that's when the worst thing ever happens:

A bird poops on my head.

T.J.

Mari is screaming her ass off.

Can't say I blame her.

A big gray glob of bird shit is on top of her head.

"Hey, hey, it's okay," I say.

She squeals. "Oh my God I'm gonna catch bird flu! And my hair!" She pulls a long strand out to stare at it. "My hair is ruined."

Sierra is laughing. Mari is yelling at her to stop. I'm biting my lips together, trying not to crack up. She's so cute.

People around us are staring.

I get to my feet. "C'mon, let's go wash it out."

With her hand in mine, we hustle down the beach to the water and wade into the lake. The cold water is a relief on this blistering July day.

Megan is exiting the lake. "What's going on?" she calls out.

"I had a bird poop incident!" Mari says, and Megan cracks up as she continues walking back to the towels.

I turn Mari around to face me. The look on her face is so aggrieved, it's adorable.

"Of all the people to poop on, why me?"

I laugh. "Here, lean your head back."

She falls backward on top of the water, her feet rising to the surface. As she floats on her back, I gently work the bird poop out of her hair. This is gross as hell, so I'm surprised I don't mind.

The sun beams down, sparkling on her wet body. Her eyes are closed and she has a little smile on her face. Her curly hair fans out on top of the water, like a mermaid. I'm straight-up ogling, but I can't help it. Not after our kisses on the beach. I want to pull her to me and never let go.

But what were she and Sierra talking about on the beach? Did Mari have something going on with one of her guy friends? I thought she said she hadn't really dated before. Is there another guy? Is that why she supposedly doesn't date? Now I'm wishing I'd pressed Sierra for more details.

If there is another guy, I need her to know I'm interested in her regardless. I'm not throwing away a chance with her.

"I'm really happy," I say. "I mean, not about the bird poop in your hair, but being here."

Mari pulls herself to a standing position, her feet sinking to the lake bed, and drapes her arms around me. Her eyes meet mine. "I'm happy too."

"I know this is only a weekend—"

"That's right," she says immediately.

I take a deep breath, overwhelmed. With her hands woven

in my hair, it's hard to think about anything right now, but I wish it could be more than a weekend, even though that doesn't make any sense. Even if I don't understand what's happening between Mari and me, I want to make sure she's not into someone else.

"What were you and Sierra talking about back there? Did something happen with one of your friends?"

She lowers her head. Slowly she begins to nod. "My best guy friend, Austin... He liked me, but I didn't want a relationship with him. It messed up our friendship... Like, we still talk, but it's not the same. It feels forced. He's upset with me, and I wish I knew how to make everything better."

"I'm sorry," I tell her, truly sad she and her best friend are in a tiff, but I'm also relieved she doesn't want a relationship with him.

"Thanks," she whispers, looking up at me from under her thick eyelashes.

She takes my hand, wading a little farther out to where the water nearly goes up to her neck. Under the surface, she wraps her legs around my waist. And I nearly have a heart attack. Mari's legs. Are wrapped. Around me.

Who knew Chicago was heaven?

No one can see us out here under the water, so I let my hands wander a little. I start at her waist, then gently roam to the backs of her smooth thighs. A gasp escapes her lips.

"This okay?" I ask.

She nods, touching her sun-warmed forehead to mine. I urge her mouth to mine, curling my body around hers, telling myself to stay in control. Remember what I'm doing. Don't need any more R-rated movie scenes out here in public.

Then her parents really would send in the Marines.

After making out in the lake for who knows how long, Mari and I go back onto the beach, shaking the water from our hair. My fingertips look like prunes.

We approach our towels to find Sierra and Megan lying together, laughing at something on one of their phones.

Sierra looks up at us. "All better? Did you get the bird poop out?"

"Yeah." Mari runs a hand through her curly wet hair. "Thanks to T.J."

We sit down on Mari's towel, sharing it. We lean against each other, her arm running the length of mine. The most surprising thing about spending time with her today is how easy it's become. Now that we've kissed, it doesn't scare me to touch her shoulder. To take her hand in mine.

It's like getting past the first kiss unlocked all this freedom to be ourselves.

My brother told me I needed to gain confidence. With her, yes, I feel surer of myself, but it's something else. Something more. I don't know if I'd be as confident with anyone else. With her, it's natural. Easy.

I pull my phone out from where I'd hidden it under my T-shirt. It's hard to see the screen in the bright sun, but I find a notification from the radio station doing the Lolla scavenger hunt. The first selfie on the hunt is the Chicago Bean at Millennium Park. I take a quick look at my phone map. While it's a quick car ride, it would take at least half an hour to walk over there.

Ethan: Things good with Mari?

Me: YES ☺

Ethan: You ask her out?

Me: She lives in TN...

Ethan: That sucks.

Tyler also texts me.

Tyler: Want to come out on Krysti's boat?

Me: I thought you were going to the concert??

Tyler: Going back later this afternoon. On the boat first.

Me: Why'd you change your mind?

Tyler: It's a boat! 🚤

Me: Can I bring Mari and her sister and friend?

Tyler: Ok

My brother texts me instructions on how to get to Chicago Yacht Club, which is south of here, but not far from the concert at Grant Park. And I'm pretty sure Millennium Park is on the way there.

I look up from my phone. "My brother is seeing this lady. At least, I think he's dating her. They invited us out on her boat. Do you guys want to come?"

Mari

A boat?!

Okay:

1. I really want to go on a boat. Seeing people out on the water always makes me hella jealous.
2. I really want to go on a boat specifically on Lake Michigan, where I will dance and drink and party. Meanwhile, people on shore will look out and be hella jealous of me.
3. Mom and Dad will ground me until I'm forty if I go on a boat with people they don't know.

"Mari, Mom will probably kill me if she finds out I'm on a boat," Sierra says, reading my mind. "And David will for sure kill you."

"You don't have to go," I say.

She gives me a look. "Are you kidding? Of course we're going. It's a boat!"

Everyone seems to throw all their principles out the window when it comes to boats. I give my stepsister a side hug, loving her so much.

"We have to be careful though," Sierra says. "No pictures or social media posts, got it?"

"Got it," Megan and I reply.

"That includes you, too, T.J." Sierra says.

He lifts an eyebrow. "Me?"

"Mom's following you now," Sierra says. "If you post that you're on a boat, she'll know we're with you."

"Why is Leah following T.J.?" I ask.

Sierra sweeps her hair over one shoulder and plays with it. "Mom saw the #HelpMariFindTJ hashtag I posted."

"Shit," I mutter. "That must mean Dad knows too."

Sierra shrugs. "I think they both feel better now that I came to hang out with you guys."

Now that I think about it, my phone hasn't been blowing up recently. Dad stopped the rapid-fire COME HOME NOW texts.

"And seeing the picture of you two together helped," Sierra adds. "Mom said that T.J. looks like, and I quote, 'the sweetest cinnamon roll.'"

I snort with laughter.

T.J. blushes and mouths, "Cinnamon roll?"

While T.J.'s slipping his T-shirt back on over his head and putting his shoes back on, I pull Sierra to the side.

"Really?" I mutter. "What's up with you talking to your mom about T.J. being a cinnamon roll?"

"I told Mom maybe you and T.J. might get together, that's all."

"Sierra, I'm here for a weekend and that's it. I'm not getting together with him. Not like that."

Without waiting for a response from Sierra, I march over to T.J. "How are we getting to the yacht club? Taking another Ryde?"

"How about we rent bicycles? You like bikes, right?"

"I do." Except for when it's raining or snowing, I ride my bike to school every day. "How'd you know that?"

He scratches his head, glancing at Sierra. "Uh, just a guess."

Has Sierra been telling him things about me? "I don't think it's a good idea to ride bikes. Not without helmets."

"You're right," T.J. replies, ducking his head. He's sweet.

Instead of bikes, Megan suggests riding electric scooters along the shoreline. It seems much safer than bikes, since you're closer to the ground and likely going more slowly.

But I've never ridden a scooter before, and, at first, I'm terrified I'm going to fall off, and a cyclist or a talented runner will smash me into the pavement, but Sierra shows me how to use it. And before I know it, we're zooming along the shore, the hot wind blowing through my hair. My skin feels sticky with sweat as the sun beats down on us.

"Wooo!" Sierra screams as her scooter zooms by a runner. Megan rides her coattails. T.J. glances over his shoulder back at me, grinning. God, he's cute. Sweet. Artistic. Unbelievably nice. How is that boy wrapped up in a single package?

On the way to the yacht club, T.J. pulls over into Millennium Park to take a selfie in front of the famous Chicago Bean. Before we hopped on our scooters, he told me all about how he wants to win this selfie contest so he can meet his favorite band at Lollapalooza tomorrow. Seems like a long shot, but I love any excuse to visit Millennium Park.

With an arm wrapped around me, T.J. holds out his phone to snap a selfie of the four of us. He tweets the picture, tagging the WTGP radio station along with the #LollaScavengerHunt hashtag.

Sierra and I go up closer to the Bean. It shines like a mirror. We pull out our phones, make funny faces, and take pictures of our reflections. Sierra loops a finger through her own Tiffany necklace the shape of the Bean. The real thing is about a thousand times bigger than her charm.

As I'm staring at my reflection in the Bean, behind me I see two girls approach T.J. He's far enough away I can't hear what they're saying to him, but he smiles and nods in response. One of the girls moves closer to him and leans in, unabashedly flirting. He glances my way before responding to her.

It bothers me.

Why is that girl talking to the boy I've been kissing today?

Seeing him smile at someone else makes me want to punch something. Surprising, considering I've never been territorial like this, unless we're talking about food. Nobody hogs the chips and salsa. But worrying about a guy? It's not something I've cared about before.

Sierra catches me staring at T.J.'s exchange with the random girl. "Do you like him a lot?"

"I don't know," I say honestly. "It doesn't matter."

"Don't you want to try dating somebody?" Sierra asks. "You gotta do it sometime."

"No, I don't."

"Don't you want to get married?"

"I'm planning to be a very cool spinster."

"Don't you want kids?"

I give her a look. She of all people knows you don't have to be in a relationship to have kids. "I'm seventeen. I'm not thinking about kids."

"I don't want you to be alone."

"I'm going to adopt a little army of dachshunds."

Her eyes dart in T.J.'s direction. "And what about hooking up or whatever? Aren't spinsters virgins?"

"This isn't the eighteen hundreds."

"You're the one who wants to be a spinster!"

The thing about high school is that some people think you have to be in a relationship to have worth, but you can be on your own if you want to. Whether or not you're with somebody doesn't determine if you have value.

"You don't have to be in a relationship to hook up," I say. "What you do with your body is your own choice."

Sierra steals a deep breath, then swipes her hair behind an

ear. She quickly glances at Megan. "I dunno... It seems the physical aspects might be better when there's a connection, or love."

Maybe for you, but I don't need that. But as I'm watching T.J. speak to another girl, I don't like it. I don't want him talking to her or anybody else—not after making out with him this afternoon. I should storm over and plant my flag in front of him.

But that's selfish of me. It's not like he's mine.

A vision of our first kiss flashes in my mind, making me weak at the knees. This afternoon I've felt close to him, both physically...and emotionally. Closer than I've ever felt before. The most surprising thing about it is I felt safe.

I shake my head. This is a weekend fling and nothing more. Did kissing T.J. take over my ability to think rationally? My pulse rockets out of control.

"Let's go take more pictures," I say to Sierra, to get my mind off these weird feelings I'm having.

That's when T.J. sets his chin on my shoulder, and gently wraps his arms around me from behind, embracing me in the warmest hug.

It's sexy, but also cozy, so I expect my heartbeat to return to safe and normal.

But as his lips gently kiss my ear, my heart beats faster and faster and faster.

T.J.

Krysti lied to me.

Her parents don't own a boat.

They own a yacht. A fucking sixty-foot yacht.

"Teej!" Tyler pokes his head over the side of the ship. He's wearing sunglasses. "Hi ladies, come aboard."

Sierra, Megan, and Mari squeal, and begin to climb the ladder and up over the side to the deck. One by one, Tyler stretches out a hand to help them aboard, and more squealing ensues. I make a mental note: Boats make girls go wild.

I climb up to find a party. Pop music blares from the speakers. I spot Mike and a woman who must be his girlfriend lounging on a vinyl side bench. Several other people are here too. A group of five people is sitting at a table, playing Uno. Krysti is at the bar, mixing drinks.

For some reason, Tyler is wearing a boat captain's hat. "I want it," I tell him.

"No can do. You'll have to wear the first mate's hat."

"Is there such a thing?"

He adjusts his hat. "Hell if I know."

"I figured you were already at the concert."

He shrugs. "I'll go tonight."

"I'm surprised you came out with Krysti."

"Me too. But I'm a sucker for a boat, you know?" He wraps an arm around me and pats my chest with his other hand. "Want something to drink?"

"Uh, sure."

Tyler walks me over to the bar area. Yes, this boat is so big it has a bar. Tyler pulls a canned beer out of a tiny refrigerator for me. Krysti is giving Mari, Sierra, and Megan pink drinks with umbrellas.

"Thanks, Krysti," they say.

"Of course. You two are such a gorgeous couple," Krysti says to Megan and Sierra, who are leaning against each other like they often seem to do.

"Oh we're not together," Sierra says quickly, and Megan gives her a sad look.

If you ask me, they're totally into each other, but neither wants to make a move.

With drinks in hand, Megan and Sierra step gingerly out onto the bow of the boat, where they lie down and sunbathe.

Mari comes over to me, sipping her drink through a straw. "Yowza, that's dangerous. Strong."

I drink my beer. "Is it good though?"

She takes another sip. "Delicious."

"It's my famous strawberry-banana daiquiri," Krysti replies, looking pointedly at Tyler, who has eyes for nothing except the boat's steering wheel. Tyler is now sitting in the captain's chair wearing the captain's hat. He looks like a little kid, playing with all the buttons.

Mental note: boats make boys go wild too.

I pray he doesn't break the boat.

Meanwhile, Krysti stares at him like she'd rob a bank if it meant she could have him all to herself.

If women always look at him like this, then it makes sense why he's confident. There's no question she wants him. No way girls have looked at me this way—I'd have noticed. Right?

Unless I was so nervous I couldn't get out of my own head.

Like the time I hung out with Sam at the company picnic and went to the city park after. How was she looking at me? I couldn't even tell you. I was too busy worrying that I was screwing everything up, that I was saying the wrong thing or doing something stupid with my hands. I never relaxed or acted like myself.

Tyler's right. I need to be more self-assured. Stop worrying. Pay attention to what's happening around me.

So I do it. I look up at Mari.

With her lips wrapped around her straw, she's staring straight at me as she sips. Her gaze sends shivers across my skin. Shit, I wish I were that straw.

I put out my hand, inviting her to sit with me at the stern on a vinyl bench. It's so hot, the vinyl sears my skin, but after a few moments I start to get used to the heat. I stretch an arm around Mari and she cozies up next to me, her head resting comfortably against my shoulder. I like the way her dark curls cascade down my arm.

We listen to the music and take frequent sips of our drinks. Out here on the blue water, with a beautiful girl at my side, I can't help but think that this is what life's all about.

I gaze down at her. She looks up at me. And I know we're thinking the same thing.

Our heads move toward each other. Our mouths meet for slow, dizzying kisses. Our lips were made for this.

My blood is on fire.

"Want to take a tour of the boat?" she whispers.

I glance around to see what's going on. Sierra and Megan are still sunbathing together out on the bow. Tyler and Krysti are dozing in the captain's chair together. Everyone else is either asleep or way too into the card game to notice us.

We climb down the stairs to the lower deck. It's carpeted, with soft lighting. The walls are shiny wood paneling. We peek around, being nosy. There's a full galley kitchen and a circular dining booth that seats four or five people. She opens a door, which turns out to be to a bedroom. I raise my eyebrows at her.

Before I know it, she pulls me through the threshold into the bedroom, then turns and shuts the door. Her fingers swiftly lock it.

My heart explodes with excitement. Sweat breaks out on

my neck. She turns, our eyes meet, and she takes a deep, shaky breath.

She walks around the tiny room, checking out the blue bedspread, old-fashioned lantern, and framed artwork of sailboats. "This is nice."

"Uh, yeah," I reply, because those are the only words I'm capable of at the moment.

I'm in a bedroom with a girl.

I'm surprised I can even speak at all. My throat closes up. I can barely breathe my pulse is racing so fast. It's so fast I can't see anything. The only thing that can bring relief is her.

Her, her, her.

After she finishes checking out the room, she turns back to me with fire in her eyes. She reaches up to push my hair to the side. Her fingers sweep across my cheek and stay there, as she gets up on tiptoes and presses her mouth to mine.

Then our hands are everywhere. I wrap mine around her waist and pull her to me, bending down to press my lips to her warm neck.

Our lips meet again and again, but her cute glasses are in the way as usual. She takes them off, folding them carefully and setting them aside before reaching for me again, pulling me to her mouth.

She breaks the kiss and laughs when I whine, but I stop my protest once I see she's lifting her top over her head. Next she reaches for my hem and then my shirt's on the floor. For a second I worry we shouldn't be doing this in somebody else's bedroom, but when our skin presses together, my thoughts are lost. Our mouths meet again for slow, hot kisses so intense they might catch fire and sink the boat.

My fingers find their way to the button of her shorts. "May I?"

She quickly nods and says, "Yes. Yes, definitely."

She leans back against the small side table and shakes out her hair. God, she's sexy. My trembling hands unbutton her shorts and ease them down, revealing the pink bikini bottoms from earlier. I struggle to control my breathing. I'm gasping for air. Her hands grip the table as she kicks her shorts off, starting a fire within me.

I might die at the sight of her body leaning against that table. My obituary will read: *Cause of death: one pink bikini.*

Above deck, music blares, the bass thumping a fast rhythm. I gasp over and over like I've been doing sprints. We begin to kiss again as I pull her backward toward the bed and onto my lap. I'm completely turned on. Hard as a rock. I worry my arousal will scare her, but she watches my face and runs her hands through my hair.

And I'm lost.

Mari

Is this a dream?

He knows what he's doing with his hands.

He knows what he's doing with everything.

It's like he can't get enough of me.

I can barely think right now, but I'm aware enough to know my body's here and my brain's gone. There's no worries at all. Just having fun and wanting more. I want, want, want.

Since he asked me before taking off my shorts, I ask him, too, and he responds by cupping my face in his hand and kissing me.

Once his shorts are gone, and I'm in his lap, my fingers glide over his strong chest. The results from the gym are spectacular. He pushes my bikini strap to the side, letting it fall. I weave my fingers in his hair, making him moan.

I can't believe it. I'm finally hooking up with somebody!

My hips move against his, his hardness pressing to me. It scares me a little, just because it's a new feeling, something I haven't experienced before. But it thrills me that I turned him on. I glance down at his boxers, excited by the tent there.

When he dips his hand into my bikini bottoms, we both hold our breath. The whole world stops.

"Do you want me to keep going?" he asks.

I nod frantically. "What's next?"

"I'm not sure. Want to figure it out together?"

"Yes, together."

With his eyes closed, he begins to move his hand against me. I clutch his shoulders tight and kiss his lips again as he teases my body until I'm dizzy, seeing spots. At home at night, under the covers, I've done this for myself, but it's nothing compared to this. Nothing. It feels like somewhere over the rainbow.

"Is this right?" he asks.

"You're great at that," I mumble, and he grins in response.

"I want more," he says, easing me off his lap, to where I'm standing in front of him in my bikini. His fingers loop through my bikini bottom strings. "This okay?"

I'm not sure exactly what he's planning, but I trust him, loving how he keeps checking to make sure we're still on the same page. I give him another nod, pulling a deep breath. I feel like I might pass out from overstimulation. He pulls on my bikini string, unraveling it. *Unraveling me.*

Then he tugs my bottoms down, pulls me against him, and trails his lips down my stomach and lower. *And lower.*

I gasp so loudly I'm sure everyone upstairs noticed. Hell, people on the International Space Station probably heard me.

T.J. looks up at me with a mischievous grin, then closes his eyes and takes me to a place I've never been. At first I'm scared, and embarrassed, but he seems into it, like he can't get enough, so I touch his hair as his mouth drives me wild. So wild I can't stand. I grab his shoulders to hold myself up.

"Here," he mumbles. "Come here." And he lies me back on the bed, where we're both more comfortable. This is the best moment of my entire life. The moment I become a woman.

Once I'm able to breathe again, I sit up. He pulls me into his arms, hugging me hard. God, this is personal, and to be honest, almost too much. I've never done that with a guy before. It seems like something you would build up to over time, but in this instance, it felt right. We wanted it, so we did it. And that's okay. But it's still intense.

I sit up and ease back from him, panting. I need to catch my breath. I'm too warm.

"Mari," he breathes, and reaches for his shorts on the floor. He digs in the pocket and finds a condom.

Hot blood roars in my ears. "T.J., I'm not sure I can do that yet."

Without another word, the condom disappears back inside his shorts pocket, and he rests on his elbows above me and resumes kissing my lips, as if it's the only thing he wants in the world.

"That doesn't mean I don't want more," I say between kisses.

He raises his eyebrows.

I kneel in front of him on the bed, reach inside his boxers

and take him in my hand, marveling at how hard and silky he feels. He weaves a hand through my hair, looking at me like I'm from out of this world. My heart begins to race again, as I lower my lips to him.

Not because he did it for me, but because I want to.

Because I like him.

T.J.

"I never want to get out of this bed."

Mari curls her body around mine. "We have to at some point. I mean, you can't just steal a boat. They arrest people for that."

"I dunno," I say, stretching my arms. "Krysti seems really into my brother. Maybe she wouldn't care if we live here from now on."

Mari looks up at me. "Does he like her a lot too?"

I play with a lock of her dark curly hair. "I'm not sure. He said he wasn't sure if he's interested in anything serious. I think he likes being single, so he can do whatever he wants."

"You mean, whoever he wants."

I laugh, loving how brazen Mari can be.

Mari snuggles against me. "I don't think there's anything wrong with it. I mean, it's not like any of us are getting married anytime soon."

I inhale deeply, my body tensing. Does this mean Mari thinks what we did together is a casual thing? I did that with her because I'm totally into her, not because I want a random hookup.

I rub my eyes. Who am I kidding? We live hundreds of miles apart. I'm coming here for college. Casual is probably our only option.

But I don't want that. Not really.

I want something deeper.

I roll over to kiss her lips again, wondering if it's too soon to ask for round two. My fingers tiptoe up her leg as she presses her hips to mine. Our feet twist together and her fingers graze my lower stomach, and between kisses she looks deep into my eyes. I take that as an invitation she wants more. I dip my hand between her legs again, and she gasps and kisses me harder.

When we're finished, we lie on our backs and hold hands. I smile up at the ceiling, happiness bursting out of me.

The words are on the tip of my tongue. *I want you. Do you want to try for something more? Maybe you could visit your dad more often. When you're here, you can come to my dorm. I like you so much.*

Shit. If I said those things, would it scare her off? Would she literally jump ship, right into Lake Michigan? A few minutes ago, we were completely wrapped up in each other. She pressed herself to me like she'd never let go. It was more than physical for me. I felt it deep under my skin. You don't do that with somebody and then jump ship, right?

And the way she was looking at me... I know she wants me.

But Sierra told me Mari doesn't do relationships.

What would Tyler do in this situation? He'd do whatever he wants. He'd tell her he wants her.

But he wouldn't be over the top about it. He'd say something smooth like, "Can I see you again?"

My heart is racing. I'm opening my mouth. I'm going to broach the subject of getting together after this weekend. Maybe she can come for fall break.

My head says I should tell her how I feel.

My heart says to shut up—it doesn't want to get broken.

I don't want her to think I'm weird, for saying how I feel when we met less than a day ago. Who does that?

What should I do? Tyler would tell me to go with my gut.

My head says that after this weekend, she's going home to Tennessee.

My gut says something else.

Tell her, T.J. Tell her what you want.

I look up into her eyes.

Mari

As I lie here in T.J.'s warm arms, I can't stop thinking how much I hate the laws of physics.

By tomorrow night, he and I will be hundreds of miles apart. If only I could walk through a portal or take a molecular transport somehow, maybe we could meet up again.

Being with T.J. is like waking up early on the weekend, cozy in bed, when you don't have anywhere to be. Nothing to do. Nothing is missing. You're simply there, relaxing, warm and happy. It's simple.

Right now? I admit... I've never felt such joy. I look up at his face to find a sexy sleepy smile. I could get used to this. And that scares me.

My racing thoughts overwhelm me, so I decide to check my phone again. Playing with the screen helps me unwind. I flick to Instagram and browse through the pictures. The vivid colors and happy smiles soothe my frayed nerves. One thing Instagram's good for is putting a pretty gloss over the messiness of real life for a little while.

My thumb scrolls to a new picture posted by Lulu Wells, a girl from my high school who graduated a couple years ago. It's a photo of her and Alex Rouvelis, her longtime boyfriend, standing by a baseball field with their arms looped around each other.

They are famous at my school for their long-running on-and-off relationship with mega highs and super lows. According to my ongoing cyber stalking, they've stayed together even while going to separate colleges—her in Rhode Island and him in Tennessee.

In the picture, Alex is staring at Lulu like she's his whole world. And from what I know of them, she is. Even though they had their problems in high school, no one would ever question that he loves her.

A niggling jealousy forms in the pit of my stomach.

Their relationship worked out, and it seems to have worked out well, but that doesn't always happen. I wonder what their secret is. Or if they even have one. Maybe if you meet the right person, things work out between you, even if you have to work through difficult circumstances.

I continue scrolling through IG until I come across the picture T.J. posted of us after we found each other last night. I let out a little sigh at the soft expression on T.J.'s face. I scan through comments from friends from high school and from lots of strangers, fangirls, and fanboys who started following us after the whole #HelpMariFindTJ fiasco last night.

At the bottom is a recent comment:

When the boat's a rockin don't come a knockin!!! Congrats Teej for getting it done!!

"Who the heck is T-Bonezzz?" I ask.

T.J. cracks up. "It's Tyler's secret Instagram account."

"What's your brother talking about?" I ask.

"Hmm?"

"On Instagram. He commented on your picture of us."

T.J. sits up, digs in his shorts pocket to find his phone and navigates to the post. His nose scrunches as he reads the comment. "Oh God. My brother is an idiot."

"His comment. It's kind of gross." I mean, T.J. and I did disappear for a while, so someone could assume that's what we were doing. Then I think about how T.J. pulled out the condom a little while ago. "Were you talking to your brother about doing it with me or something?"

T.J.'s face begins to boil red. He leans over onto his knees and rubs his eyes. "I mean, of course I wanted to—you're beautiful." He doesn't say another word. He's staring at the floor.

"T.J.?" I ask. "You okay? It's all right, I'm not upset about your brother's silly account."

He lets out a deep breath and rubs his eyes again. "Mari?"

I look over at him. "Yeah?"

"I want to see you again."

"Yeah, it sucks I'm going back to Tennessee tomorrow, or I'd definitely want to do this with you again too. That was amazing. So are you."

His eyes widen, and that small, sexy grin reappears on his

face, and I wonder how long I have to wait before reaching for him again.

But then he quickly shakes his head. "It's not like that. Not sex, I mean... It's something different? Something more?" He lies back down next to me and looks at my face. His strong gaze is like looking into a blinding sun. "Maybe we could hang out when you visit your dad again? And talk online? Get to know each other better?"

Did he just rocket from zero to sixty? I open my mouth to speak, then close it again. I bite my lip.

As he watches me, his face clouds over with disappointment, and my heart pangs with guilt and hurt for him.

This is why I don't want anything serious, so no one experiences pain. I went for the weekend fling to keep things simple, but I guess it wasn't simple for him.

I thought I was clear.

"I'm sorry, T.J." I say, quietly, and as gently as I can. "I don't want a relationship. Not with anybody."

He shakes his head. "I wasn't asking for a relationship, Mari. I only asked to see you again."

"But why do you want to see me again?" He implied he wants more than fooling around. "You want it to lead to something more, right?"

He musses his hair and fidgets. "I don't know. I wasn't trying to make some big thing out of this. I like you, that's all."

He likes me.

Again, that joy bubbles up inside me, threatening to spill over into a smile. It's as if T.J.'s rewiring my insides.

Losing this feeling will suck. I can't get drawn in any more than I already have.

We only met yesterday. Just because we've gotten along today doesn't mean it will continue.

"I've had a great time with you today," I say softly. "But this was only supposed to be a weekend, right?"

He purses his lips and sits up straight. "Yeah, sure." His voice is agitated. Angry, even. "I don't understand why you seem so anti-relationship, though."

"Because they don't work out, T.J."

He narrows his eyes at me. "C'mon, plenty of people have good relationships."

"Yeah, maybe. But for me, it's not worth it. Look what happened with my best friend." My voice shakes. "I wasn't interested in him, and it messed everything up. It sucks. And look at my mom? She lost my dad, and now she's bitter and mean. I don't ever want to become like that." My personal words spill out of me, and I instantly regret sharing them.

T.J. swallows hard. "Isn't it good that you know those things, though? You can look out for them."

"There's no guarantees, T.J. Deep down, I think you are who you are, and that doesn't change."

"You really don't ever want to date anybody?"

Why'd he have to go and ruin everything by starting this conversation? "I'm sorry, but I'm not interested."

He faces me straight on and boldly lifts his chin. "You're scared."

T.J.

Without a word, Mari stands up.

She reties her bikini and adjusts it back into place. With swift hands, she grabs her jean shorts off the floor and puts them on.

"I should go," she says without looking at me.

I slide off the bed to hop to my feet. "No, wait."

Mari gives me a small smile, sweeping her hair behind her ears. "I had a really good time with you, T.J."

"Me too. With you, I mean." I run a hand through my hair, pulling on it. "Can we pretend I never said anything? Go back to where we were?"

She slides her glasses on. "We can't go back... We're in different places. I don't want to hurt you."

You already are, I think. "C'mon, Mari. Stay?" I try not to sound like a creepy beggar, but it's impossible. I remember what Sierra said about always having snacks on hand. Maybe she's not thinking straight because she's hungry. "Want to grab something to eat?"

She swiftly shakes her head.

"Please?"

Her face crumples as she leaves the room to climb the steps. After yanking my swimsuit back on and pulling my T-shirt over my head and shoving my arms through the holes, I rush after her, hot on her heels.

For years I've wanted to meet someone and now I have and she's disappearing in front of me, like a fading dream.

Once back above deck, the sun flashes in my eyes, blinding me temporarily, but once I can see again I notice she's looking everywhere but at me. She walks over to the bow and calls out, "Sierra? Ready to go?"

I'm panicking. I don't know what to say to get her to stay.

Her stepsister and Megan gather their towels and stand, being careful not to fall on the boat deck. With furrowed eyebrows, Sierra gazes back and forth between me and Mari.

"Where are we going?" Sierra asks.

"We're leaving," Mari says, taking Sierra's arm.

"Thank you," Sierra tells Krysti. "This was a lot of fun."

"Best strawberry daiquiri I've ever had," Megan says, and Sierra elbows her. "Okay, it's the only one I've ever had. But it was the best!"

"You're welcome," Krysti says brightly.

"Guys, can we go?" Mari says, and even though I don't know her all that well, I can hear the panic in her voice, and it makes my heart clench for her. I want to call out to her, to try one more time to get her to stay, but I don't want to distress her any more than I already have. So I stay silent. And it kills me.

They climb off the boat. I lift my arm to wave bye to her. She glances over her shoulder one last time.

It can't end this way. She ducks her head and walks off with Sierra, who turns to give me the evil eye. I don't deserve that.

I put myself out there. It's Mari who won't even try.

My heart is crumbling.

"Is everything okay?" Krysti asks me.

"No."

Krysti gently touches my forearm. "Is there anything I can do? Do you need to talk?"

If I hadn't listened to Tyler's advice, maybe this wouldn't have happened. I wouldn't have spooked her. Maybe she would've stayed.

I go over to the captain's chair, where Tyler is leaning back with the captain's hat draped over his face.

"Tyler."

I touch his shoulder to wake him up.

He lurches out of the chair and stumbles to his feet.

He must think I'm goofing around, because he pats my chest and rubs my head, like he likes to do, as if I'm some damned little kid. "Teeeej."

I shove him off me. "Stop."

"Hey, hey, what's wrong?" He glances at my hands. "You need another beer?"

"No, I don't need another beer." I can't believe she left. "Shit."

Tyler focuses on my face. "C'mon, man. Calm down. What's wrong?"

"Mari left."

Tyler looks around the boat. "Oh, that sucks. What happened?"

"I told her I want to see her again."

Tyler gives me a nod like he's impressed. "Good for you."

"Turns out it's not what she wanted, and left."

Tyler sips from his beer cup. "It's okay. You'll meet plenty of other ladies. It'll be easier now that you have some experience."

I haven't told Tyler a thing about what happened between Mari and me, but he just automatically assumes he knows. He always thinks he's right. Thinks he knows what's best. If I hadn't listened to him, put myself out there, she wouldn't have left.

And now he's trying to get me to move on to someone else, like it's no big deal. To me, it is a big deal. It's a big fucking deal.

"Don't you get it? I'm not you. I wouldn't use a girl like that."

His eyebrows furrow. "I don't use girls," he spits. "It's always mutual. I'd never hurt anyone."

"What about Krysti? She wants to date you, and you're just stringing her along."

"That's bullshit." He whispers to me, "I've been straight with her the entire time about what I want. It's her who keeps looking for something that's not there."

"Doesn't stop you."

Tyler gets to his feet, his chest to mine. It occurs to me then how much bigger he is. How much stronger. My initial instinct is to run and jump overboard, but I puff out my chest and confront him. This is important.

"Teej, this is none of your business."

"You're always up in mine. I don't want to be like you."

For the first moment since we started this conversation, Tyler's giving me his full attention. He stares at my face.

"You're always telling me what I should and shouldn't do," I say. "I never get to decide for myself."

"If you'd grow some damned balls already, I wouldn't feel like I had to give you so much advice."

"I never asked you."

"That's just it. You do. You ask me what to do all the time. You never figure anything out on your own, Teej. I don't give a shit what you do or don't do. But you have to do something on your own. You're not living."

"I'm living!"

Mike is suddenly between us. "C'mon, guys. You've both had a bit to drink. Let's relax."

Tyler pushes Mike out of the way. "Are you living, though?" he says to me.

"You never know when to let up," I snap. "Always telling me what to do so I don't embarrass you."

"You don't embarrass me. Don't put this on me." Tyler's face is contorted with anger. Or is it pain? "I knew it was a mistake to invite you here."

"What?" My voice chokes.

"I thought you were grown up. I thought you'd stopped acting all pathetic. I guess not."

I need to get off this boat. I turn around to find Krysti standing there, tears in her eyes. I feel terrible. She's been nothing but nice to me, and I'm a complete dick.

"I'm so sorry," I tell her. "Thanks for having me. Uh, see ya."

With lots of people on other boats staring at me, I quickly climb off Krysti's and quickly walk up the dock, looking for anywhere else to be but here.

Mari

"You need something to eat."

"I'm not hungry," I tell my stepsister, even as my stomach rumbles.

"Yeah, nobody believes that," Sierra says, making Megan giggle.

Sierra and Megan are leading me along the lake path toward Dad's apartment. Without the scooters, it'll take a while to get there. We're far away.

But I don't think I could ride a scooter again right now after walking away from T.J. My hands are shaking. I'm biting down on my lip. This stupid day is overwhelming.

"Let's at least stop to get some water and sit down for a few minutes," Sierra says. "It's too hot out. You'll get sick."

We leave the path and go up to the Chicago Riverwalk, where Megan leads us to a cafe she likes that serves sandwiches, burgers, and salads. Now that I see the restaurant, I think I'd literally die for a Diet Coke with ice. Inside, people occupy a few tables, but it's mostly empty: the lunch crowd is gone, back to the beach or shopping or Lollapalooza.

A hostess shows us to a wooden table adorned with a small bouquet of wildflowers. As I slide into my chair, I've never been so happy for air-conditioning. It cools the sweat on my forehead. I touch my face with the backs of my hands; it stings. I have a sunburn.

This isn't what I figured I'd be doing today. When I imagined visiting Chicago for Lollapalooza, I pictured going out with Sierra and her friends and dancing to music with thousands of other people. Strangers.

I didn't imagine I'd meet someone who flipped me inside out.

This whole thing with T.J.—he's such a nice guy. And that feeling when we were lying in bed together? I loved it. It could be addictive. It's like how I can't play only one game of Tetris on my phone. One game ends, and my brain itches for another.

But even if I did want more, it's not like he and I have any chance of being together, not when we live so far apart. There was no reason to go down that road. I did the right thing.

As I think about him and his cute, mischievous grinning face and how much I enjoyed simply being with him, a physical, tingling pain shoots through my arm and to my heart.

I make my mind go black and drown the pain in darkness.

While waiting on the server to come over and greet us,

Megan checks her phone. "Sierra, Dad is buying White Sox tickets for next weekend and asked if you want to come."

Sierra makes a face. "I've told you before, there's no way I'm going to a Sox game. Ever. It's sacrilege."

Megan rolls her eyes. "The Cubs aren't the only game in town."

"Yes, they are," Sierra says. "The only way I'd go see a Sox game is if the Cubs were ripping them to shreds in the World Series."

Even though I'm not feeling my best, I can't help but snicker at them acting like an old married couple.

Once we've ordered drinks, Sierra touches my hand. "What happened?"

Megan raps her knuckles on the wooden table. "Do I need to go back and kick some T.J. ass?"

I shake my head. To change the subject, I open my menu and scan it. "What do you all want for lunch?"

Sierra pushes my menu down. "Mari, what happened with T.J.?"

I'm not sure if I'm ready to answer that. I've always enjoyed girl talk. Back home, Rachel and I tell each other everything, especially when it comes to guys. But I'm not sure if I'd tell even her about what T.J. and I did specifically. It's the kind of personal thing you don't even write in your journal—you never tell a soul because the emotions, the memories, are too raw.

Luckily, I don't have to answer Sierra's question about T.J. because the server chooses that moment to place a glass of Diet Coke full of ice in front of me and passes out drinks to Sierra and Megan. "What can I get you to eat?"

Sierra's right; I need food. When I don't eat, I become an uber crankypants. It's so hot outside, though, it's killing my appetite. Scanning the menu I choose a chilled watermelon gazpacho and a mixed salad. When the server leaves to put our order in, Sierra presses me again.

"T.J. What happened with him?"

I lean over onto the table, rubbing my face with my hands. "After we made out, he got all serious. Started talking about how he wanted to see me again."

"Yes!" Sierra says.

Megan drums her hands on the table. "That's good! I knew he really liked you." She pulls her phone out of her bag, dismisses her Chicago White Sox screensaver, flicks to the first photo Sierra took of us, and holds it up to where we can all look at it. "I'm so jealous."

Megan staring at our picture reminds me of how just a little while ago, I was studying that photo of Lulu Wells and Alex Rouvelis. Something about their picture made me jealous too.

I've never been interested in having someone that's all mine. Now, suddenly, it's on my mind. T.J. is right—sometimes it works out with a couple, but how do you know if it will? And that's just it. You don't.

"I don't like him like that," I say, trying to play it off, so they'll leave the subject alone. "Good hookup, though."

Megan looks from me to Sierra, and they gape at each other.

Why does everything have to be such a big deal?

I change the topic. "So, you guys liked those strawberry daiquiris? Did you see how Krysti made them? We'll have to remember so we can do it ourselves. I mean, if we can get the rum somehow."

I look up to find Sierra sipping her Coke, watching me with wide eyes. She sets her drink down and sighs, looking defeated. I don't see why she cares so much. My life isn't hers.

Megan sweeps her braids over a shoulder and leans across the table toward me. "You don't like T.J.?"

"Nope."

Lie.

Yes, of course I like him, but I'll have to get over it.

Will I ever forget the look on his face when I left him behind on the boat? It was like Austin all over again. I hate that I hurt both Austin and T.J.

I'm a movie villain.

Megan focuses on our picture again. "Mari, look at you guys." I wish she'd stop doing that. I should steal her phone and delete all the social media apps so she won't do it again. "You wanted each other from the very beginning."

"I agree," Sierra says, and gently touches my hand. "If you really don't like him, that's one thing, but I don't want you to miss out on something because you're so set against falling in love."

"You don't get it," I snap. "Your life is happy. Your mom got my dad, and my dad left us, and now I'm stuck living with a mom who yells all the time. If you had any idea, you'd stop pressuring me to do something I don't want to do. People don't have to be in relationships. It's okay not to be in one. Now can you just drop it?"

Avoiding my eyes, Megan picks up her water glass and hides behind it, taking long sips, covering her face.

Sierra's eyes are watering. She swipes a tear away. And now I feel like a total jerk for making the best person in my life cry.

"I know I'm lucky," Sierra says with a shaky voice. "And that I have a good life. It's just that I want you to be happy too."

Sierra's phone buzzes and the screen lights up. Mom calling. Mom calling.

With another swipe at the tears in her eyes, Sierra storms off with her phone to talk outside. Meanwhile, the server drops off our plates. The sight of their burgers and fries makes me wish I had gotten comfort food. I need dessert ASAP. Not that I deserve it. Not after hurting Sierra.

While she's outside, Megan watches her through the window and ignores me. I don't blame her. I shouldn't have raised my voice.

Sierra comes back into the café and slides into her chair.

"I'm sorry for snapping," I say quietly.

Sierra arranges her napkin on her lap, not looking at me, and takes a long gulp of water. "Listen, Mari... Don't get even madder, but Mom and David really want to see you, so they're coming here."

"Nice, they can pay for our food," Megan says. They bump fists and smile at each other.

"Shit," I mutter. "They're totally gonna tell me off."

Sierra bites into a french fry. "It's better here than at home. They're not going to yell at you in public."

"With my luck today, it just might happen."

About ten minutes later, Dad and Leah arrive. She sails over in her red sundress and gives Sierra a kiss on the cheek and hugs Megan's neck. Leah turns to me with a short smile, but doesn't greet me like the other girls. Dad pats me on the back, seemingly unable to even look at me.

I wince at Sierra, who won't look at me now either.

A server pulls another table up to ours so we can all sit together. Sun shines through the windows, but it feels dark in here.

Leah studies my face. "You got some sun today, Mari. Are you burned?"

"A little," I say quietly. My skin—especially on the top of my head and upper back—is hot and sore. I forgot to reapply sunscreen after we went in the lake to clean the bird poop out of my hair.

"Make sure to drink lots of water." She pushes a glass toward me, and I take it gratefully and begin to drink. Yeah, I'm seventeen years old, but I like being taken care of and fussed over, especially when I feel so drained.

Leah is looking around the restaurant. "Mari, where's the boy you met? T.J.?"

"With his brother, I think," I say as calmly as possible, not wanting to give Dad the impression he was right, that I shouldn't have run off with T.J. today.

"I'm glad you're okay," Dad says to me, jerkily removing

the silverware rolled up in his napkin. "Until Sierra found you, I was worried. I didn't know where you went."

"Of course she's okay," Sierra replies. "It's Chicago, not a war zone."

Dad gives her a look as he steals a fry off her plate. "Mari doesn't know Chicago like you do. Because she never comes to visit. And when she finally does, she decides to run off with some strange boy and worry us all sick."

Dad is angry, but I can also hear the hurt buried deep in his voice. At the moment, though, it's hard to care. I'm hot, sunburned, confused, and my heart hurts like hell.

I bury my eyes in the heels of my hands. "If you ever bothered to visit me, or even ask how things are at home, you'd know I can't visit you."

I hear gasps around the table, but I keep on ranting: "All you care about is your life and want me to fit into it, when there's no way I can. Not that you and Leah understand. Everything's perfect for you. But for y'all to be happy, I have to be miserable. Don't you get that?"

The waiter approaching the table takes one glance at me and turns around and vamooses. Leah's rubbing the side of her neck, while Dad's face is blazing red. Sierra wipes another tear away. Megan reaches out and takes Sierra's hand.

This trip was a mistake. A mistake on so many levels.

I yank the napkin out of my lap, throw it on my plate, and rush across the restaurant toward the exit.

"Is everything okay?" the server exclaims.

"Gazpacho's great!" My voice breaks as I'm pushing the glass door open.

"Mari!" Dad calls out in an exasperated tone.

Outside, a tear drops down my face. And then another. I bite my tongue to distract myself, to try to stop crying. Around the corner is a staircase leading down to the river. I go down a few steps, then decide to sit. I've always thought of myself as strong and in control, but today? I feel like I've lost everything.

Seconds later, Sierra settles beside me, loops her arm around mine, and leans her head against my shoulder. "I'm sorry you're hurting," she says, and I give her a nod, happy she's with me, but embarrassed about my outburst all the same. A lot of people would write me off after I blew up like that.

We sit like that until Dad appears on my other side, standing above me.

"Sierra, can I talk to Mari for a few minutes?"

Sierra squeezes my wrist. "Text if you need me and I'll come back out here."

"Ladybug." Dad slowly sits down next to me, folding his hands. "What did you mean in there? That you can't come to visit?"

I wring my fingers together, thinking about physics again. In another universe, maybe I'm sitting here on the steps enjoying a day out in Chicago with my dad. In that life, Dad is pointing across the river at the Chicago Tribune building, which I've always loved because the walls are decorated with rocks, like from Roman ruins and the Great Pyramid at Giza.

In another universe, I'm still at home with Mom, too afraid

to have visited in the first place. In a million other universes, different things are happening.

But in my perfect universe, Dad never left, Mom didn't lose the baby, and everyone's happy, including me.

"I can't visit because it upsets Mom when I'm with you."

Dad gives me a weird look. "But you're my daughter."

He's clueless.

"Mom isn't happy, you know. I don't think she'll ever be happy again."

Dad rubs the top of his head. "I know she's unhappy. And I wish I could help, but only your mom can figure out what makes her happy. I tried, Ladybug. I tried so hard to help."

Did he really though? He never encouraged her to try therapy. Never did anything. He shut down. "You left me."

"I never *left* left you," Dad says. "I called you every night."

"You stopped calling—"

"Because you hardly ever picked up," Dad snaps. "Do you know how bad that hurt? After a while, I couldn't do it anymore. I couldn't stand not talking to you."

I stopped answering because Mom got angry when I talked to him. Plus, there was nothing he could say to make things better at home. What was the point?

"I hurt, too," I say.

"Let me help now," Dad insists. "Come visit more often. Let's figure things out."

"You never came back, Dad. All you cared about was me coming to visit you here."

"It seemed like you didn't want to come."

"Of course I wanted to, but I couldn't. Even coming this weekend is too much for Mom. She's going to be pissed when I go home."

Dad touches my shoulder. "I'm sorry she'll be upset. She'll get over it though."

He doesn't get it. But telling him more would mean betraying Mom. It might get her in trouble. I can't tell him about Mom's mood swings. How she screams at me all the time. How she yanked my ponytail so hard I thought I'd lose my hair.

Dad goes on, "You're my daughter. Home is with me, not just your mom."

This is it. The opening I was looking for. "Next year, I'm thinking of going to college here."

"That's great."

I see him thinking, his eyes shifting around.

"What is it?" I ask.

"Have you, uh, thought about scholarships?"

"Yes, and I have Poppy's trust fund, and maybe I can take out a loan."

Dad audibly exhales.

"But room and board," I add. "They might be expensive." I take a deep breath. "While I'm here, I was going to ask about possibly staying with you next year."

Dad smiles a little, but then a frown works its way onto his face. "We can talk about it. I need to check with Leah first, to get her thoughts. She owns the place."

That is a detail I didn't know. It's her apartment?

More tears blur my eyes, because that is not something I expected to hear. Does Dad have any part in it? Doesn't he help with the mortgage or rent or whatever?

"I want out of Manchester so bad," I tell him. "I'd move here now if I could."

"What are you saying?" Dad asks softly.

"I'm saying, I wish I could stay here. I don't want to go back."

Back to a mom who yells all the time. What if she does worse than pull my hair?

Dad bites the tip of his thumb, staring straight ahead. While I'm waiting for him to answer, a riverboat passes by. The more time that goes on, the more my heart sinks.

"I'm not sure if it could work right now," Dad finally says.

"Because there's no room for me at the apartment?" I snap. "Leah doesn't want to give up her perfect guest room?"

He jerks his head from side to side. "It's not that. Don't be silly."

"Then what is it?"

"It's the custody agreement. Your mom has custody of you until you're eighteen."

My eighteenth birthday is in March.

Dad goes on, "You can visit me, but only on weekends, and for two weeks each summer. That's what we worked out in the deal."

"So change the deal."

"I'm not sure if I could sue for custody. Your mom would fight back like the first time... The divorce already wiped out nearly all my savings." He grips the back of his neck. "I'm sorry, this is all embarrassing to talk about. I wish I had more money."

"So you won't even try?" I whisper.

Dad's head droops. "I don't think it makes sense when you're turning eighteen in less than a year. It would cost too much."

I tried. I wanted to be something other than second best. I put myself out there, and still, my parents put themselves first.

He looks over his shoulder back toward the restaurant. To where his new family is waiting for him.

I get to my feet. "Forget it."

I rush down the steps.

"Mari!" Dad shouts, but I keep on moving.

I jog the rest of the way down the stairs and toward the bridge, unsure where it leads.

T.J.

Going to Lollapalooza for the first time. Hanging out with my brother. Seeing my favorite band in person.

This was supposed to be the best weekend of my life.

Now I'm wandering downtown on Michigan Avenue—the shopping district—in my swimsuit.

I could go back to the beach, but it'll only remind me of Mari. I should go back to Tyler's place, but I'm not sure if he's there, or if he even would want to see me.

I pull out my phone and text Tyler:

I'm sorry I blew up like that.

When I first started yelling at Tyler, it felt good. Relieving. I had so many frustrations pent up inside. But the more I kept talking, everything came out worse and worse. The hurt look on Tyler's face keeps repeating in my mind. Yeah, I don't like how he's always telling me what to do and I hate what he said about how I'm not truly living, but I went too far. I'm an asshole.

Tyler doesn't text back. Tucking my phone back in my pocket, I wander around the Chicago Tribune tower, which always reminds me of a tall, skinny Gothic castle, with its elaborate spires reaching toward the sky. I distract myself by looking at the famous rocks on the walls. There's a piece of metal from the World Trade Center, which fell before I was born.

I can only look at the rocks for so long. I feel like I should be doing something else, but what?

I leave, and wander down crowded Michigan Avenue, weaving around pedestrians carrying shopping bags—some hurrying, while others lazily walk and gaze in store windows.

Down the street, I peer into the Apple store. It's packed with customers troubleshooting problems with their MacBooks and iPhones. I'm tempted to fake an issue with my phone, so I can go in and lick my wounds in the comfort of air-conditioning.

Maybe something is honest-to-God wrong with my phone—it still hasn't buzzed with a notification from my brother.

It scares me that Tyler hasn't written back. Normally he's attached to his phone like a lifeline.

I wander up closer to the river, to lean across a railing, gaze at the water and watch riverboats inch by.

I was right when I told Mari she's scared. But I barely know her. I shouldn't have pushed. It's just, when I was lying there in bed with her? She felt worth every risk there is to take.

Okay, so I've never done that with a girl before, but to me, it wasn't simply a physical act—I felt more there. Something deeper. Something that made me throw all my usual hesitations out the window.

All this time, I never noticed that hesitation protects you from the possibility of being hurt. I don't tell my brother I made these leather bracelets, because I don't want him to question or make fun of me.

Instead, I hesitate, and don't say anything. It protects my feelings.

But with Mari today? I told her everything. I pushed past my fears.

When you meet someone you like enough to push past your hesitations, that's where the possibility happens. That's where the risk comes in. And it didn't pay off for me.

Still, moving past the unknown is like removing a heavy weight from my chest. It's hard to explain, this sense of freedom you get once you're open with a person. It's almost like after a first kiss. You're free to move on and accept whatever comes next. You're free to fly.

I can't help but tilt my head back and smile up at the sun.

My watch buzzes on my wrist. I rush to look at the notification, to see if it's Tyler.

He sends a three-word response: Go cool off.

I rub my cheek. Lean up against the railing, pray my knees don't give out.

Tyler's never been mad at me before. Then again, I'm still pissed at him for telling me I can move on to someone else, like what happened with Mari was no big deal. But I miss him already. What if I screwed things up so bad he doesn't forgive me?

My smartwatch buzzes. I immediately glance down at it, hoping it's Tyler again. Or maybe even Mari.

But it's not. It's the WTGP radio station with another #LollaScavengerHunt prompt. At first I think, *Who gives a shit?* I don't feel like doing anything. But then I think of how much I want to meet Adam Tracy and ask about his cover designs. Maybe learn something from him.

Plus I have a lot of time to kill before my bus leaves tomorrow night.

I glance at the tweet. This time they're directing us to take a selfie in front of the lion statues outside the Art Institute of Chicago. I check the map on my phone, and it's not a long walk from here.

I set off across the bridge.

Mari

After that awful conversation with Dad, I hurry back down toward the river.

I don't know what it is about water, but it makes things better. It may not solve your problems or tell you what to do with your life, but at least the gentle blue calms you. Some of my best memories are from walking along the beach during a sunset, excited about getting back out there the next day for another round of swimming and sunbathing.

But today? I'm not excited for tomorrow. I take off my glasses, and dab at my watering eyes with the heel of my hand.

I decide to try to video chat Austin. It's loud out here on the bridge with the traffic zooming behind me, but everywhere in Chicago is noisy. This will have to do.

I open up the messenger app and press on his picture. He answers a few seconds later. It looks like he's outside in his backyard.

"Whoa, whoa, whoa. What's wrong, Bud?"

I'm crying now and it's hard to speak. "Bad day," I choke out.

"Hold on a sec." Austin starts walking with the phone, angling it toward the blue sky. Suddenly he's inside and moving down the hall to his room. Once he's sitting on his bed, he turns his phone back to focus on me.

"What happened?" he asks.

"Just got into a fight with my dad. It was bad."

"That really sucks." Austin leans back against his bed's headboard. "What can I do?"

I shake my head, not sure what to say. I should tell Austin more about how I asked Dad to move here, but I imagine the idea of me moving would upset him, and I don't want to hurt my best friend even more than I already have.

"But other than that, are you having a good day? Based on Instagram, it seemed like you were having fun at the beach with T.J." Austin's voice is interested but hard at the same time. It's like he wants to be nice about T.J. but is hurt too. I don't blame him.

"I ended up leaving T.J. behind a little earlier."

"Why?" Austin growls. "Did he hurt you or pressure you or anything?"

"No, no. Nothing like that. We just wanted different things."

Austin pauses for a bit before speaking in a flat voice. "He likes you, and you don't want to give anyone a chance."

I wipe my nose on my hand. Gross. "Why would you think that?"

"Mari, you're funny and beautiful and nice. Any guy would want you. You're just so hardened...so closed off from everybody, you won't put yourself out there."

"It's my decision."

"And I think you're going to regret it in the long run."

Another tear falls from my eye. I need to change the subject. "What are you doing today?"

"Getting ready to go four-wheelin' with the guys."

"Be careful, all right? You know how much I hate those death machines."

Austin laughs. "You'd love 'em if you gave 'em a try, Bud."

My phone begins to beep. *Mom calling. Mom calling.*

"Listen, I gotta go," I tell Austin. "Call you later?"

"Yeah, talk to you tonight."

Austin's face disappears from the screen, leaving only Mom's flashing number.

After this horrible afternoon, all I want is to feel better. Maybe I can tell Mom a bit about what happened. I think back to how Sierra curled up against Leah's side last night and find myself wishing I could do the same with my mom. For now, a phone call will have to do.

The second I hear her voice, I wish I hadn't answered.

"Where the hell do you get off, telling your father I won't let you visit him?"

Oh no. Dad must have called to confront her. Why would he do that? I guess it's a good thing I didn't tell him anything else. He would've blabbed it to her. To hurt her, to get back at her. And in return, she'll make my life hell when I go back home tomorrow.

I speak slowly: "I didn't say that... Dad got mad because I hardly ever come here. I told him it's hard to visit because I don't want to leave you."

"Your dad thinks I'm keeping you from him. I don't stop you from visiting. That's a lie."

I take a deep breath. "But, Mom, it's true that you don't like it when I come here."

"I've never said that. You can visit your father anytime you want. You know that."

I hate it when she does this. When she defends herself, saying she didn't do something she obviously did. "Mom, you called me a traitor and wouldn't drive me to the airport."

"I never said that."

Sometimes I think I should record our conversations and play them back for her. She'd probably deny it was her voice. She's a master class in gaslighting.

"I told you this morning," Mom barks, "I don't want to talk to your father on the phone. You keep stirring shit up there, and he keeps calling to complain about you. If he calls one more time while you're there, you'll regret it."

She hangs up on me.

I rub my eyes. I let out a little cry, wishing I could live with Sierra and go to school with her and learn physics in Spanish, and not have to worry about someone who gaslights me.

I want a mom who cares, who takes care of me. In that

moment, alone on the busy bridge in Chicago, I realize it's never going to happen. I'm stuck with who I've got. It's my destiny. Nothing will change. And it's so unfair.

Dad texts me: Please come back.

I can't even with him right now. Not only did he run straight to Mom, he told me he won't fight for me, that I'm not worth the money.

A tear rolls down my face. I swipe it away.

An older woman and man avoid looking at my face as they hurry by. A guy in his twenties rushes past like I have a disease. I don't even know what to do or where to go.

I've never felt so low. So lost.

Then I hear a voice: "Are you okay?"

T.J.

The universe is out to get me.

I'm walking across the bridge, heading south toward the Art Institute of Chicago, when I look across the lanes of traffic to see her.

Mari.

Of all people.

Pacing back and forth, talking on the phone.

What are the odds? How many millions of people live in Chicago?

I stop walking and stare. Look around to see if there's somewhere I can hide. What if she sees me? Will she think I'm following her like Asshole Bob?

In the next moment, she wipes a tear from beneath her glasses and puts her phone away. She removes her glasses and covers her eyes with a hand.

My feet move before my brain says go. I jog up to the

crosswalk, wait for traffic to stop, and then dart across the street. Where's Sierra and Megan? Why is Mari all alone?

I approach her slowly. "Mari?"

She looks up at me in shock. She quickly averts her gaze, touching her cheek. I see now that it's pink. She's sunburned. Ouch.

I feel an overwhelming urge to pull her into my arms, like earlier today, but that would be too much. I won't scare her off again like I did before. Still, even thinking about what we did on the boat makes me feel shook up inside.

It was the best moment of my life until it wasn't.

"Are you okay?" I ask.

She shakes her head. "I'm thirsty."

"I was just heading down to the art museum. Want to walk along? We can find some water on the way."

I expect her to say no, but she slides her glasses back on and gives me a quick nod, as if the fight's drained out of her. Which surprises me, because I found her so confident and sure up until now. What happened?

I want to take her hand so badly, to show I'm with her. Instead we walk side by side in silence, with the sounds of the city playing in the background. A plane roars overhead, music spills out of a car window.

As we leave the bridge and continue on Michigan Avenue, places to eat and convenience stores come into view. *Snacks.* I need to get her snacks. And then I see it. Something bound to make her feel better, no matter what's wrong.

"C'mon," I say, and lead her to Garrett's Popcorn.

"I love this place," she mumbles.

"I know."

She looks up at me as we fall into line, her big brown eyes staring deep into mine.

We go inside the store. The air-conditioning chills the sweat sticking to my skin, making me shiver. Various kinds of popcorn fill big glass cases. I scan the menu. I had no idea there were so many flavors. Buffalo ranch popcorn? Macadamia? Is the video game we're living in glitching?

I stick my hands in my pockets. "What's best to get here?"

"I love the caramel and cheddar mixed together. It's a classic."

At the register, we order water and popcorns. I take her suggestion and choose the cheddar and caramel, even though the caveman deep inside me is scoping out the buffalo ranch.

When it's time to pay, I pull out my debit card. Mari tries to pass her own card to the cashier, but I wave her hand away. I made plenty of money landscaping this summer. Out of the corner of my vision, I see Mari narrowing her eyes in confusion as she puts her card away.

The cashier slides us two bottles of water, while another worker hands us two wax bags filled to the brim with popcorn.

Outside, we carry our food and drinks a little way down the street to a park with trees, where we can sit in the shade. As we walk, a few pieces of my popcorn fall out of my overflowing bag and bounce on the ground.

It's hard to believe we were right near here earlier today, when we went to the Chicago Bean. My whole life changed in a few short hours.

Once we're sitting safely on a bench, she gulps a bunch of her bottled water, then wipes under her puffy eyes with a forefinger.

I pull a handful of popcorn from my wax bag, push it in my mouth, and chew.

"Do you like it?" Mari asks.

"I love the cheddar." I dig out another piece of it and eat it. "The caramel is good, but kind of sugary for me."

She plucks a piece of caramel from my bag. "I'll eat it if you don't."

Things went downhill with her earlier, and I'm nervous as hell right now—I don't want her to leave, but my happiness at being with her overpowers any other feelings. I give her a tentative smile.

She steals more of my popcorn. Then wipes her eyes again.

"Do you want to talk or anything?" I ask.

Mari opens her own wax bag, pulls a couple of pieces out, and eats them hungrily, then sighs. "It's been a tough day."

"I'm sorry. What happened?"

Mari pops a few more pieces of caramel popcorn into her mouth.

With another deep sigh, she speaks. "My parents... I asked my dad if I could move here."

My heart races at the idea of her living in Chicago. "What'd he say?"

"That Mom has custody, and he's not willing to fight for me."

I scrunch up my face. Why wouldn't he fight?

"Why do you want to move here? Aren't you a senior? Don't you want to stay at your high school with your friends?"

"Mom... She's getting worse, not better." Mari's voice shakes. "It's like she's filled with so much hate for my dad—for what he did—that it's eating her up. She's unrecognizable, you know?"

I don't know, but I nod along to show I support her.

"What do you mean it's getting worse?"

"She yells so much, T.J. It's awful...and—" She closes her eyes. "The other day, she got so mad I was coming here, she pulled my hair."

I've never heard of a mom doing something like that. I've heard of parents hitting their kids and abusing them, but pulling her hair? What is that?

"Did it hurt?" I ask.

She toes at a pebble on the ground. "A little maybe."

It may not have hurt her physically, but she's clearly torn up about it. "Did you tell your dad about this?"

"I don't want to get Mom in trouble. She's already had to deal with so much..."

"That means you know what she did is wrong."

Mari crinkles the bag in her hand. "Nothing's going to change. Dad doesn't have money to fight a custody battle for me. He said he doesn't think it's worth it."

"But does he know she hurt you?"

"It was only the one time."

From what I understand, if someone hurts you once, they'll hurt you twice. They'll hurt you again and again. If she pulls Mari's hair, is it possible she'd do something worse?

"But what about your feelings?" I ask. "She yells at you. That can't be easy to live with."

Mari shakes her head.

We sit in silence chewing our popcorn. I can hear her phone blowing up. *Ding. Ding. Ding.*

"Your phone," I say. "Somebody's texting."

"It's probably Sierra. Or Dad. I don't know. I just can't right now."

I pull my phone out of my pocket and open the DM from Sierra, the one where she gave me helpful tips. I quickly type to her: Mari's ok. She's with me.

Sierra types back: Thanks! ☺ Will tell her dad she's ok.

After that, Mari's phone stops beeping.

"Thank you for the water and popcorn," Mari says, getting to her feet. "I'd better go—"

"Stay." I say it before I even think. "Stay with me. Please."

Mari

"Stay."

"T.J., I don't know if I should—"

"I don't want to be alone right now," he says quickly. I don't think I've ever heard a boy say something like that before. Most of the guys I know keep their emotions folded up and tucked deeply away, hidden under their cowboy hats.

I'm a complete jerk—I've been so preoccupied with my own messy life, I didn't notice that T.J.'s not himself either. At least, not how he acted earlier. His face is all scrunched up in pain. His hair sticks out in all different directions. Has he been pulling on it?

I sit back down on the bench and face him. "Are you okay?"

T.J. eats more popcorn, then shrugs. He leans over onto his knees and looks at the ground. "I got into a fight with my brother. It was... It was bad." T.J. rubs his cheek. "I have no idea what I'm going to do. I should just go home to Madison. I don't think I can go back to Tyler's tonight."

"He's your brother. He won't kick you out."

T.J. shuts his eyes. "He doesn't want me here. Said it was a mistake to invite me."

Oh, that's a terrible thing to say. It must have been a bad fight, because I never got the impression Tyler was mean like that. To me, it seemed like they love each other and have the kind of family I wish I had. Frankly, it seems like T.J.'s whole life is blessed, with his art skills, sense of humor, good looks, and acceptance to the University of Chicago. Maybe T.J.'s life is not what it looks like on the outside?

It reminds me of seeing a gorgeous sweater in a store, only to try it on and discover the yarn scratches your skin. Was I too quick to classify T.J. and his life?

I reach over and touch his arm. He folds his hand on top of mine. It feels warm.

"Do you think Tyler overreacted?" I ask.

T.J. shakes his head. "I'm not sure. We both said mean things, but maybe it had been building for a while."

"What's the problem?"

"That's just it. I'm not sure... I'm not sure of anything."

I squeeze his arm. "You can talk to me, if you want."

T.J. leans back against the bench. Instead of responding, he chews his lower lip.

I'm so worried for him. At that thought, I sigh. Less than a day ago, I didn't even know T.J. existed. Now I care for him. I hate seeing him sad.

I'm still dazed by what happened physically between

us earlier—how intense it was. But before that, we had great conversations that kept on flowing. We were on our way to being friends.

I eat the last of my popcorn and ball up my wax bag. "You said you were walking to an art museum?"

"Yeah, the Art Institute. I need to take a selfie for the radio station contest."

"Can I go with you?"

His eyes light up a little and he gives me a small smile. "Yeah. Let's go."

We walk in silence through Millennium Park, with a couple of feet between us. The space feels wrong. My hand itches to take his in mine. My brain is saying no, and my body tells my brain to shut up.

A smiling couple holding hands passes by. A mom and dad push a baby stroller down the sidewalk. A completely bonkers shirtless man is out for his run in the hot midday sun.

"I'm glad you stayed, but why did you?" T.J. asks quietly.

"I'm worried about you."

"After you ran away earlier, I figured I'd never see you again." He drags a hand in his hair. "I mean, I'm glad you're here, but it's confusing, I guess."

I lick my lips, working to choose my words carefully. "I like you. I want to be your friend."

"Like Austin?"

It's a harsh dig, and yeah, I probably deserve it on some level, but I'm not gonna take it.

"That's not fair," I say. "I was never anything but a good friend to him."

T.J. nods slowly. "Sorry, that was a dick thing to say. Shit, I keep saying dick things today."

"Me too."

"I'm not normally like this, I swear," he says.

"Let's blame it on the heat. The heat makes us act like dicks."

We laugh together softly. Our eyes meet, and I look away.

A few minutes later, we arrive in front of the Art Institute, with its big green lions on guard out front. The museum looks like a fancy palace, like something you'd see in Paris, not in downtown Chicago. Its traditional white columns are the opposite of the shiny modern Chicago Bean.

We start to climb the stairs.

"What did you and Tyler fight about?" I ask.

T.J. takes a sharp breath. "A bunch of stuff."

"What started it?"

He climbs a few steps before answering. "I've always wanted to be like Tyler. But it turns out there are some things I don't like about him, and things he doesn't like about me." He cringes. "The fight... It was bad..."

I reach out and squeeze his arm, giving him an encouraging look, to show him I want to hear more.

"I was so mad, I said things I shouldn't... I accused him of using women." He drags a hand through his hair. "I'm such an asshole."

"Yikes, T.J. Did you apologize?"

"I texted him. Said I was sorry I blew up. He told me to go cool off."

I touch his forearm. "Let's do that. Let's work on taking selfies for the contest."

T.J.'s gaze moves from my hand up to my face. "Thanks for listening. It's nice, not being by myself."

He helps me feel better too. Simply talking with him about my problems helps me not feel so alone. And surprisingly, the issues with my parents didn't scare him off.

It's almost like T.J. is sharing my burdens.

T.J.

A green lion looms in the background.

I put an arm around Mari, aiming my phone at us. I snap the picture and we check it out on my screen.

I burst out laughing. My hair is a disaster, full of cowlicks. Her skin is pink. Our clothes are crumpled like we've been sleeping in them for days.

"We look awful," Mari says with a laugh.

"I'm tweeting it anyway."

"No, don't," she squeals, reaching to steal the phone out of my hands. I hold it up above my head where she can't get it. She jumps up, reaching for it, laughing. But I'm too tall. Then she brings out the big guns.

She tickles the shit out of me.

"Ahhh!" I yell as she laughs her ass off. I grab at her fingers, but she keeps on tickling my ribs. I tickle her sides, making her squeal.

People walking by give us weird looks. Probably not what they expected to see at the Art Institute: two filthy teenagers wrestling over a phone.

We're both out of breath, panting from the tickling and exertion. She wins my phone and shoves it in the back pocket of her jean shorts.

"Let me tweet the photo," I beg. "I really want to meet If We Were Giants. Please?"

She slides the phone out and points at me with it. "You owe me big-time."

I tweet the picture along with the necessary hashtags and tag Mari's handle in it. Since last night, I have all these new followers who immediately start liking the picture and commenting on how cute we are.

I click on the #LollaScavengerHunt hashtag to see what kind of competition I'm up against. As I scroll through the posts, I discover that not only do I have competition, but it's good competition. Two people have dressed up in those inflatable dinosaur costumes for their selfies. Two ladies are decked out in Chicago Cubs tees and hats. And then there's me, the guy who looks like he's been hit by a tornado.

So much for being creative.

I glance at my watch. It's 6:45 p.m. So much of the day is gone. My weekend is half over.

"Now what?" Mari says.

I pull up the radio station's Twitter account to see if they've posted any other landmarks, but they haven't added anything beyond the Chicago Bean and the Art Institute lions. What will the next landmark be?

We aren't far from Lollapalooza. I can hear the music blasting from here. "Since no other clues are posted yet, you want to go back to the concert?"

She adjusts her glasses, pushing them up her nose. Mari looks at me from under her eyelashes. "We could do that."

Together we walk to the Michigan Avenue entrance of Lollapalooza.

The roaring crowds and deep thump of a bass buzz my skin. My mood turns electric. Electric like anything is possible.

I'm with Mari again. Now only if my brother was here. I swipe my phone on and open the text app. I start a message to Tyler, then delete it. Then start over again.

Me: I'm at the concert. Can I come find you?

Tyler: With my buddies tonite. See you later.

I slowly slide my phone into my pocket. My brother abandoned me in Chicago. I'm still angry with him for his Instagram comment, and I guess I had some resentment I needed to get out, but I wish I had chosen my words better. Will he ever forgive me?

Without thinking, I reach out to take Mari's hand. The moment our fingers intertwine, I drop her hand and pull back. "I'm sorry. I reached for you without thinking."

"It's okay." She tucks her hands in the back pockets of her jean shorts.

It's been an emotional couple of hours. I wish I could hold her hand, but maybe I should just be happy we're together.

We make our way through the crowds to the show of Said the Sky, an EDM DJ I like. The smooth music flows like water lapping over rocks. The sun is setting into an orange-gold horizon as a slow electronic song begins. The sensual music slows the crowd down and everyone begins to sway. The light show is a kaleidoscope of dreamy silvers and blues.

Mari and I start to dance again, and it's still as easy as last night. As the crowd presses in around us, I wrap my arms around her from behind, to keep her safe. But that's all. I won't go further than that.

We haven't talked about what happened on the boat earlier. If I hadn't run into her on the bridge, would I have ever seen her again?

After today, my confidence is shot.

If she wants me, she'll have to make the move.

Mari

I've always considered myself an okay dancer.

Not good enough for the cheerleading squad and certainly not the dance team, but I can keep a rhythm and not make a fool of myself at school dances. But with T.J., my body moves instinctively on a base level. If I danced like this all the time, I could be a Titans cheerleader.

As we dance and dance and dance, it's hard to tell where my body ends and his begins.

T.J.'s smartwatch lights up. He checks the screen. "Here's a tweet from the radio station," he says over the music. "The next landmark is Centennial Wheel."

"That big Ferris wheel at Navy Pier?"

He nods. "You up for going over there?"

"Yeah. I've never been to it before."

Together we head for the exit, dodging people chugging beers and jumping up and down. Once we're free of the concert,

I take a deep breath. The city beyond Grant Park is busy with people out for Saturday night, but quiet in comparison.

It takes us about ten minutes to walk over to Navy Pier. Along the way, T.J. and I chatter about nothing. He walks with his hands tucked in his pockets. Part of me wishes I could reach out and take his hand in mine again. Earlier today I would've done it, no question. But now? After our experience on Krysti's boat? Touching his hand might electrify me. Make me do something I'm not totally ready for, and give him the wrong idea.

Arriving at Navy Pier, we come upon a rideshare drop-off area, where people are pouring out of cars and others are hopping in them to leave. We weave through a bustling crowd toward the middle of the pier. My arm brushes against T.J.'s, and he glances at me sideways.

We pass shops and restaurants on one side and boats on the other. A fresh breeze whips up the smell of lake water. Now that the sun has set, the temperature has dropped, but there's still a sticky summer night heat.

T.J. gestures up at the giant Ferris wheel. "This looks like a good place for a picture."

He's right. Surrounded by sparkling lights and joyful laughter, being here feels like a dream.

"Will the picture turn out good online?" I ask. "The sky is dark and all."

He gives me a withering look. "If there's one thing I'm good at, it's taking selfies."

I lean against T.J. for the picture, and he clears his throat before snapping a photo of us. We hover over his phone to examine the selfie. Our hair is still a disaster and our skin is shiny, but we're smiling and the lights behind us don't drown us out. It's cute.

"You are good at this," I say. "You could make good money teaching people how to do this for their Instagrams."

"We should take one onboard the wheel too."

"You want to ride it?"

"Might as well, as long as we're here."

T.J. uses a debit card to buy us tickets, and then we fall into line to get onboard.

"I've never been here before," I say.

"Neither have I. I've been to Chicago a bunch, but there's so many things I haven't done. I guess I can when I'm in college. I mean, if I have time."

We inch forward in the line. "My aunt always says college was the best time of her life. Like, she had all this free time to do things she wanted. Which I think was mostly hooking up with her boyfriend."

"Really? What about all the homework? And finding a part-time job and stuff?"

I shrug. "Maybe it depends on what you're studying?"

"Since I'm majoring in business, I'll probably have to study all the time like I did in high school. I sucked at math and statistics. I'm dreading doing that for four more years."

I furrow my eyebrows. "Why are you majoring in business then?"

"It's what Tyler did. My parents expect it."

"Is that what you want?"

"No," he says quietly.

On my wrist, I play with the bracelet he gave me earlier. The one he made. "I loved your tattoo design. And your bracelet. Do you have anything else to show me?"

T.J. swipes on his phone and navigates to the picture gallery.

I watch as he swipes up over and over again through lots of pictures. I spot him with a bunch of friends. I'll have to ask about them.

He shows me a watercolor painting he did of his dog and another of Madison City Hall. "I think this is the one that won me Most Artistic at graduation."

He knows how to paint and is clearly talented. "It's pretty."

"It's boring," he replies.

He pulls up a picture taken at night. It's a bright green alien painted on a concrete wall.

"Graffiti?" I ask.

After a glance around us at the other people in line, he nods.

I elbow him. "You're such a criminal," I tease, and he gives me a nervous smile in return. "I love your alien. It's much better than your city hall picture."

"Most people would consider that city hall painting to be real art. The kind of print you'd buy and hang in your house as decoration."

"Unless someone wants an alien painting. I love it. I want a print for my wall."

He turns off his phone screen. "You don't care that I did this?"

I lean against his side. "I mean, I don't want you to get caught and go to jail or anything, but graffiti is much better than a boring blank piece of gray concrete."

He lets out a long breath. "Thank you."

"Thank you for showing me your alien. Does he have a name?"

He nudges me. "Want to name him?"

"Yes! His name is Dave. You need to paint Dave a girlfriend. Or a boyfriend, if that's how Dave rolls."

A smile edges onto T.J.'s face. "Okay, I will when I get home."

He tips his head back and looks up at the night sky. "Do you ever worry about living the wrong life?"

"What do you mean?" I ask.

T.J. scratches the side of his neck. "It's something I think about. Every choice you make leads to something else. So if you make one wrong choice, it could lead to more choices that are wrong for you. It could set you on path where you're living in the wrong town with the wrong person doing the wrong job, all because you made one wrong choice to start with... What if I end up living somebody else's life?"

His scary, real words make my eyes cloudy with tears. They hit home hard.

Based on my parents' divorce, I've avoided relationships because I didn't want to feel hurt or cause someone else pain.

I've let fear dictate my choices. What if following the fear leads to something much worse? Wouldn't it be better to be in control of my life?

Science has taught me to use evidence to make decisions. Before today, all the information I had told me that it's better to be alone. And then, this afternoon, I truly was alone. Alone on a bridge with no one. I've never felt so terrible. Then T.J. appeared and lifted my spirits.

I made a choice to open up, to let someone else help carry my troubles, and deep down in my gut, it feels like the right decision.

I want to live based on my choices. Not based on other people's experiences, but on my own observations.

It's my life. But do I have the courage to risk it?

Now I'm wondering why T.J.'s thinking about this. He must have big decisions to make. Maybe he's been wrestling with them. And suddenly it hits me. He's struggling with his future.

"T.J.? Why wouldn't you major in art or something? Why business?"

"I don't know if I can change my major at this point. I'd have to check with my adviser at school. And Mom, Dad, and Tyler say the job market is so bad, I need to make sure I have *good, transferable skills*, so I'll always have a job. Business isn't going away."

"Neither is art. People have loved it for thousands of years. They aren't suddenly going to stop wanting it."

"I've never thought about it that way, but you're right..." He slowly turns to face me straight on, and searches my eyes. "People will always want art."

We look out over the city of a million lights.

We're in a Ferris wheel pod with five other people, but it's not crowded. Still, T.J. and I sit close together, our thighs touching.

"Want to do the selfie?" he asks.

"Sure." I cozy closer against his side and smile at his phone screen as the wheel rotates in a giant circle. It's slow, but at the same time impossibly fast. I don't want this night to end. I don't want to go back to my real life.

I gaze around at the other people in the pod. A couple older than my grandparents are excitedly pointing at the dome of the planetarium. Another couple—two men—is pointing at the shore, but they keep stealing glances at each other and laughing at what the other says.

One man appears to be alone, simply gazing out at the water. Who is he? Is he in the city alone on business, with his family back home somewhere? Is he single? Whoever he is, he seems deep in thought. Is he lonely?

I'm loving this experience of soaring above the city, but for me, it's better having T.J. to share it with.

The man checks his phone and scrolls on the screen. For a second, I'm happy because maybe he heard from his family, or a friend, but then I remember this afternoon. Even when my phone was blowing up with texts from family and friends, I had never felt so alone.

I sigh and shut my eyes.

"I'm sorry," T.J. says suddenly.

"For what?"

"About earlier?" T.J. whispers. "On the boat? I'm sorry if it was too much too soon."

I swallow, rubbing my palms on my thighs. My face is burning up, and not from the sunburn. "I'm not sorry about what we did—I wanted to do that with you... I really liked it." He peeks at me sideways, raising his eyebrows. "But I am sorry I ran off like that. You're right—I got scared."

"You were right, too, about me asking to see you again. I wanted it to lead somewhere. I've never had a girlfriend, and I want one." He cradles the side of his neck with a hand. "I like the idea of having someone to share things with. Sitting on the couch watching a movie. Going on a bike ride."

"Riding a giant Ferris wheel?"

"That too." He grins. "Whatever really. As long as it's together."

"Do you want to find dinner together after this? Lou Malnati's?"

He squeezes my wrist. "I'm in."

I lean against his side, wondering if the right person is worth a whole lot of risk.

I have no idea what I want for the future or what it holds, I only know I don't want this to end.

I breathe in this moment.

———

After spending the evening wandering around Navy Pier with T.J. and eating dinner at Lou Malnati's with him, he orders a Ryde to my dad's place and rides along with me up to the Gold Coast. In the back seat, I inch my hand over, cover his hand, and squeeze.

He looks over at me and squeezes back.

When we arrive in front of the apartment building, we climb out of the car and stand under a streetlamp. A group of people dressed for clubbing passes around us, continuing on down the street.

I gather my messy, curly hair and pull it to one side, over my shoulder. "I might see you tomorrow at the concert?"

"I hope so. I'll text you when I'm there. Maybe we can meet up to say goodbye."

I get up on tiptoes, wrap my arms around his neck, and kiss his cheek. He pushes my hair away from my forehead and gazes down at me. I press my cheek against his chest and inhale deeply.

It's easy to imagine doing this with him again. Spending the day at the beach, followed by food and a movie. Going home and losing ourselves in each other.

"Hey, listen," he says quietly. "Uh, I know it's none of my business, but I hope you'll do what's best for you. Whatever that is. If that's telling your dad what's going on at home with your mom, or not telling him. Whatever you need."

We hug again and he buries his face in my hair.

Holding me.

Supporting me.

Just being there.

After waving bye to T.J. one last time, I spin through the revolving glass door into Dad's apartment building.

The air-conditioning chills my skin after being out in the hot summer air all day. I don't want to go upstairs, but I have to. With a deep breath, I steel myself and head toward the elevator.

Suddenly the concierge steps into my path, blocking me. It's Jason, the same doorman from last night.

"Excuse me, can I help you, young lady?"

"My dad lives here. I'm going to his place."

"I'm sorry, I can't let you in without clearance."

Clearance? "Yesterday you saw me with Sierra Lavigne. She's my stepsister."

"Do you have a key fob?"

"No..."

"Then I have to get the okay from the unit owner before I can admit you to the building. Please give me a moment." With a huff, he picks up the phone and dials a number.

Unbelievable. Does he think I'm some sort of potential robber or criminal?

I roll my eyes.

You'd think, if Dad truly wanted me to visit here more often—wanted me in his life, he'd have given me a key fob. He would have told the doorman I'm allowed in because I'm part of the family.

After a quick conversation on the phone, Jason the doorman

ushers me to the elevator. I push the button for the tenth floor and knead my fingers together.

The elevator ascends way too quickly. When the doors open to Dad's floor, I'm halfway tempted to stay on and keep riding up and down until someone makes me leave. Can I live in this elevator?

I'm scared Dad will be mad. Worried he'll say I can't live here next year while I go to college. But do I even want to live with him? I'm still pissed he won't fight for me. I simultaneously want to cry and kick the shit out of Asshole Bob.

The elevator dings. The doors slide open. Slowly I step out into the hallway and approach Dad's door, preparing to knock but not quite ready yet—*gotta amp myself up*—when it opens. Dad stands in the doorway, wearing a polo shirt and khakis, waiting for me.

Shit.

"Mari? Are you okay?"

I give him a quick nod, trying to keep the expressions off my face. All my anger from earlier bubbles up and threatens to spill out of me.

He steps aside, allowing me to come in.

"Mari!" Sierra rushes from the doorway of her room and throws herself at me for a hug. "Are you feeling better?"

"Much. Thank you." I hug her back. "I'm sorry I yelled at you."

She waves a hand as if to say no big deal. "I'm sorry I was overbearing. Megan says I have an issue with that and need to watch it."

I smile at the fact Megan tells Sierra what's what.

Leah walks up, carrying a glass of white wine. She's wearing comfy-looking sweatpants and a matching velvet hoodie. Her face looks shiny, like she just washed it and went through a fancy skin-care routine. "Hi, Mari. Did you have a good day?"

"Today was good. Went down to Navy Pier tonight. I love it there."

"I do too," Leah says encouragingly, even though I've heard Sierra refer to it as a tourist trap on more than one occasion. "We should go sometime."

"Leah, Sierra," Dad cuts in. "I need to talk to Mari alone for a few minutes."

Sierra gives me a quick smile.

Leah touches my arm and speaks quietly in my ear. "I hope we get a chance to visit more later. I know you're upset, and I want to listen."

Tears well in my eyes as I give her a quick nod. Her voice and face are sincere. She's telling the truth—she wants to hear what I have to say. Maybe even take care of me. But given everything that's happened with my mom and dad, it's hard to imagine letting my guard down with Leah. She's been welcoming, but she's not innocent in all this either. It's hard to look past that.

After accepting a glass of ice water from Leah, I follow Dad into the living room. School pictures of Sierra and me are displayed in the entertainment center next to the TV.

I'm completely pooped and want to sleep, but not yet. Not

until we talk. I sit down on the couch next to a soft throw blanket. I want to wrap it around myself like a cocoon.

Dad slowly lowers himself to sit next to me. He leans over onto his knees. "I'm disappointed you ran off like that today."

"I'm sorry I left y'all at the restaurant, but I was pissed."

"Leah said you might be overly upset because you're sunburned and need rest."

Seriously? "I wasn't upset because of my sunburn, Dad. I was upset because I tried to tell you something... I was trying to say I needed you, and you sat there and said you don't have the money to help me. That sucked."

"We can talk about college—"

"I'm not talking about college, Dad. I'm talking about now."

He raises his voice. "And I wish I could help now, but I can't. It is what it is. Your mom has custody and I don't." He throws his hands up.

"It's so hard living there with Mom. You have no idea," I whisper. "You don't even care."

He rubs his cheek. "Of course I care. But what can I do?"

"I already asked you earlier today. Let me come live here. You said you wouldn't consider trying to win custody of me."

When my voice cracks, he leans over onto his knees, rubbing the back of his neck. He can't seem to look me in the eye. "I'm sorry, Ladybug. It doesn't make sense though. You turn eighteen in March and you're graduating in May. It's less than a year."

I look around this living room. It's clean and well kept. Leafy green plants calm the room. It's a place where a family gathers to have a good time. My mind flashes back to that horrible Christmas Eve, the one where Mom yelled at me constantly, as if it was my fault, as if I could do something to change our situation.

I still don't want to betray my mom, but I'm sick and tired of being second best all the time. T.J.'s right. It's time to take care of me.

Time to make a choice. The right choice.

I need to tell my dad what's going on.

"You said you're disappointed in me," I say slowly. "I'm disappointed in you too."

He recoils.

I take a deep breath. "You're the one who had an affair. You're the one who did the bad thing, yet you were rewarded with this great life. And mine is hard. You and Leah haven't even apologized for what you did."

My voice cracks, and Dad rubs the back of his neck, looking at the floor. The tips of his ears turn red. Good. He needs to know how their actions hurt me.

"Things suck at home," I go on. "Mom yells all the time. I never know what's going to set her off. She's nice when I wake up for breakfast, but by lunch she's a different person. Sometimes she even blames me for your divorce, *which doesn't even make sense*, but it still hurts. She talks... She talks about how she wishes she wasn't alive anymore."

That makes Dad sit up straight. He laser focuses on my face.

"When I said I was coming here to visit this weekend, she got so mad she pulled my hair," I say through teary eyes.

Dad sets a hand on my shoulder. "Did she hurt you?"

"I mean, yeah. It was scary." This is the first time I've admitted that to anyone. Even myself.

It scared me.

Dad moves his hand from my shoulder to my arm. "Why didn't you tell me things were so bad?"

"You never asked how Mom is. I figured you didn't care. And coming here only makes things worse with her. If you're making me go back, then I need to figure out how to soften the damage somehow, if she'll even pick me up from the airport."

Dad makes a face. "Why wouldn't she pick you up?"

"Seriously? After everything I just told you, what makes you think she'd act normally enough to pick me up? She wouldn't even drop me off to come here—she called me a traitor. Austin drove me."

A tear slips from my eye. I've heard that sometimes a divorce is the best thing parents can do for their kids, but I don't understand that. I'm caught in the middle. I'm the one suffering the most. And my parents can't even see it because they're so focused on their own problems and feelings.

This section of the city is full of green trees, fancy apartments, brick town houses, and quirky storefronts. When you're surrounded by so much beauty, it shocks when gray reality seeps back in.

I stand up to go to bed. "I'm tired. Good night."

Dad reaches out to take my hand. "You're not going back tomorrow."

"What?" I slowly sit back down on the couch.

"You can stay here longer. Under the custody agreement, you're allowed to stay here two weeks."

My heart sinks to the floor. "Dad, two weeks doesn't mean shit. If I stay here for two weeks, that's just gonna piss off Mom more. It'll make things worse."

"No, no. You misunderstand me." He drags his palm over his mouth. "I need to talk to a lawyer."

I hold my breath.

"I can't make any promises, but I can give you two weeks here. I'll talk to my brother and your grandparents, to see if they might be able to help me out. Let me see what I can do."

I give Dad a big hug. I don't totally feel safe yet, but I feel hope.

Two weeks. I can do that.

I cross my fingers that he'll be able to figure something out.

As I tuck myself into bed and listen to "Destiny," I rest my head on the pillow, thinking about the meaning behind the lyrics: whatever is meant to happen will happen, that nothing can change destiny.

I still love the song, but maybe there is a way to change your destiny.

Just step up and ask.

SUNDAY

T.J.

It's nearly one o'clock in the morning.

Tyler hasn't come back to his place tonight.

I'm lying on his couch under a blanket, my feet dangling off the cushion, trying to sleep, but it's not coming. I need to see him. To make sure everything's okay with us.

My phone beeps. A direct message notification pops up. It's from the radio station!

WTGP: You won our Lolla selfie contest! Please come to trailer 67 at 11:00am at Lollapalooza tomorrow to meet the members of If We Were Giants. You can bring a +1.

Holy shit! I jump up off the couch. The blanket falls to the floor. I get to meet my favorite band! I get to meet Adam Tracy and maybe ask him about his art.

I can't believe I won. I snort. I mean, I would hope so considering how much time Mari and I spent going around and taking selfies. The radio station sends along a little map showing me where to go, along with instructions on how to pick up an extra bracelet that will get me backstage.

Me: I'm in! Thank you!

WTGP: Please let us know by 9:00am your full name and the name of your +1 so we can put you on the list.

Me: I will get back to you shortly.

At the same time, the radio station tweets out to its followers that @TJ_Clark2003 won the backstage tour at Lollapalooza. They also retweet that awful picture of Mari and me in front of the Art Institute, the one where our hair is sticking up everywhere. It makes me laugh.

I can't wait to tell Tyler I won. He can be my plus-one.

I text him: Where are you?

Tyler: Out. Won't be back tonite. I'll see you when you come back for college. I need some time.

He needs time away from me?

I'll never admit this to anyone, but tears sting my eyes when I read his words. I need to see him. To say I'm sorry. Guess that's not happening anytime soon. Did I fuck up our relationship for good?

The radio station direct messages me again: We saw you and your friend Mari trending on Twitter this weekend. Can you bring her as your +1? We want pictures of you guys backstage!

Oh. They want Mari. For publicity, I guess?

I fluff the pillow under my head and try to clear my mind—to erase the humiliation, so I can sleep. I focus on the darkness behind my closed eyes.

The dark turns to bright vivid colors. Splatters of paint.

I can't stop thinking of that Obama graffiti I saw this morning. Next to it was this big open swatch of concrete. Sun shined down through the grate above it, almost like a spotlight. My fingers itch to fill that space.

I want that spotlight on my work.

On my art.

———

I text Mari, asking her to come backstage to meet If We Were Giants.

It's late, though, so I don't end up hearing back from her until I wake up the next morning.

Mari: Invite your brother. Not me. I don't even know this band. You know he'd love it.

She's right. I have to at least try.

I text Tyler: I won this contest. Get to go backstage to meet If We Were Giants.

He doesn't respond immediately, hopefully since it's eight o'clock in the morning and not because he never wants to speak to me again.

I decide to get in the shower. When I'm out, I towel off my wet hair and see a blinking light on my phone. A notification. I swipe on my phone screen.

Tyler: No shit, really?

Me: I can take a +1. Will you come with me? Please?

I hold my breath, waiting for him to respond.

Tyler: Where do I meet you?

I'm waiting at a bagel shop on Michigan Avenue.

Tyler agreed to meet here before we walk over to the festival. Because food.

A mix of excitement and dread go to war inside me. I can't wait to go backstage and meet my favorite band. But the idea of seeing Tyler again freaks me out.

Other than fighting over Xbox controllers and who gets the last piece of garlic bread at dinner, we've never had a real argument before. I'm not sure what happens next.

Through the glass window, I spot him coming up the street. I bite my cheek. Tyler pushes open the shop door and gives me a single nod. He has circles under his eyes and he's wearing the same clothes he wore yesterday.

Without a word, we stand in line and look at the menu. It's written in English, but none of the words register for me. I'm so nervous and worried the words look like a foreign language I don't know.

By the time I step up to the cashier, I have no idea what they have to eat much less what I want to order.

Tyler steps up to the register. "Two everything bagels with cream cheese. Orange juice. Coffee please."

"Two of those, please," I say. I don't think I've ever had an everything bagel before. Does that mean literally everything? Even dirt? It might end up tasting like dirt for all I know, but I don't care right now. All that matters is making things right with Tyler.

I pull out my debit card. "Let's pay with Dad's money."

"Now we're talking, Teej."

Once we have our food, I follow Tyler over to a small table by the window.

"I'm sorry," I tell him.

"Don't give me that shit," Tyler says, dumping cream in his coffee. "You meant every word."

Red hot blood rushes to my face. To cover my embarrassment, I gulp down some of my orange juice.

"I'm glad you said it," Tyler adds. "It sucked what you said and it pissed me off. Really fucking pissed me off." He stops to take a big bite of bagel and chew. "But I'm proud you had the courage to say it."

"I could've said it nicer."

"That's for damned sure." Tyler rips off a piece of bagel. "You hurt Krysti's feelings a lot. She's pretty pissed right now."

"I didn't think you cared about that? I mean, it doesn't seem like you want to be serious with her."

"Dude, I met her less than three weeks ago." He chews his bagel. "I'm twenty-two. I'm not about to get married. But that doesn't mean I want to piss off the woman I'm seeing. Or hurt any woman. Besides, who knows what might happen with Krysti? We got a pretty good thing going on. Or, at least we did."

I am so confused. I have no idea what Tyler wants. Is that what happens after college? You have no idea what you want?

It's strange to me, that Tyler doesn't know exactly what he's doing. I always thought he was in perfect control. Maybe he's just like me? Along for the ride and figuring things out as I go?

"I can text Krysti to tell her I'm sorry," I offer.

"I'll tell her," Tyler says.

We chew our food and look out the window. A man and his waddling bulldog pass by.

"Things are okay with Mari," I tell Tyler.

"Did you get back with her?"

"I mean, we hung out last night, but nothing else happened. We danced, that's it. I don't know if she'll give me another chance... She's not really into dating. Ball's in her court now."

Tyler sighs. "I'm sorry, man. About what I said about how you'd find someone else. It's just that I think it's good to talk to lots of different people to figure out what you want."

"What if what I want is one person?"

"You can like whoever and whatever you want. You're you and I'm me. If you don't agree with me, tell me to fuck off, and that's fine."

I always thought Tyler wanted me to act a certain way. Did he pressure me because I myself wasn't stepping up to make my own decisions?

"Listen," I say carefully. "I want to get a tattoo, but not a hula girl."

Tyler bursts out laughing. "A hula girl. What a stupid idea."

"It was your idea."

"I know, and it was stupid as shit. Thank God we didn't go do that. Mom would've killed us."

"I actually do want a tattoo." With a deep breath, I swipe on my phone screen and scroll to my design. I pass it over to him.

He takes my phone, holds it closer to his eyes, and studies it. "Wow, this slams."

I burst out laughing at his words. I find them so incredibly dorky, but he likes the phrase, and he owns it. It's him.

It doesn't matter what other people think or if you're worried something is silly or nerdy. If you like it, you like it. You own it.

I need to own what I love. Be openly proud of it, no matter what anyone else thinks.

"I designed it," I tell Tyler.

"Sh-it," he says, his eyes focusing on it again. "You could make money designing tattoos like this."

"I want that," I say slowly, carefully. "I've been thinking of changing my major. To graphic design or art or something."

He doesn't look away from my design. "What about business?"

"Ty, I hated taking stats. I don't know if I can live through four more years of math."

His eyes grow wide as he looks up at me. "I had no idea. Why didn't you ever say anything?"

"I guess I hoped someone would ask or figure it out. I mean, I won Most Artistic at graduation and in the yearbook."

Tyler laughs. "Shit, man. I don't take those awards seriously. I mean, in the yearbook, I won Most Spiritual."

"Uh, why?"

Tyler tilts his head while he thinks. "I was always talking

to girls about their horoscopes. They were really into it. Talking about Mercury in retrograde and stuff."

"Hey, Mercury in retrograde is nothing to laugh about," I shoot back.

"You're the most spiritual person I know, Teej." He drinks from his juice carton. "You're seriously thinking about majoring in art?"

"Yeah."

"If that's what you want, I'm behind you."

"Really? Won't it embarrass you?"

Tyler gives me a look. "It won't embarrass me. And even if it did, I told you. Tell me to fuck off and that's the end of it."

"I want to major in art. Maybe minor in graphic design." I chew my bagel for a long moment. "Mom and Dad will kill me."

Tyler waves a hand. "I'll have your back. They might be okay with it once they see you're serious. What else have you designed besides that tattoo?"

I swipe on my phone again. With shaking fingers, I find my little green alien. The one Mari called Dave. I show the picture to Tyler.

I hold my breath as he stares at the alien while chewing his food. "That's awesome... Maybe don't show that one to Mom and Dad, though. They'd probably send you to art rehab or some shit."

Mari

Sierra is hogging the bathroom mirror.

"C'mon," I whine. "I need to put on my makeup."

She sets her eyeliner down and checks her smartwatch. "We're fine. We've got time."

"I'm supposed to get breakfast with Dad before the show."

"Oh! Change of plans. Mom and David are taking us both out for food before we head to the concert."

That's good, I guess. Eating with my dad won't be so awkward if Sierra's there.

While I brush on my primer, Sierra weaves her hair into a long braid. By the time I'm done with my mascara, Sierra's still working on her foundation. You'd never know she's getting ready for a day at a festival. You'd think she's preparing to shoot a movie scene.

This is going to take a while, so I go out into the living room to wait for her, and find Leah sitting on the couch, drinking coffee and scrolling on her phone. When she sees me, she sets her cup and phone on the coffee table.

"Mari! Good morning."

I sit down in a chair across from her. "Good morning."

I rub my hands on my thighs and send telepathic messages to Sierra telling her to hurry up already. Before this moment, I've never been alone with Leah.

"Did you sleep okay?" she asks.

"Yeah, it's a comfortable bed. Thanks."

Leah smiles. "If you want to pick out another comforter and some different wallpaper or paint, let me know. Sierra says the guest room reminds her of a vampire's funeral home."

I giggle at Sierra's brashness.

"Sierra and I don't share the same taste," Leah adds.

"Me neither," I say. Sierra's room is all bright reds and oranges. I prefer softer colors—those pastels T.J. totally hates.

"If you can give me an idea of what you'd like," Leah says, "I can pick out new decor before you visit again, or we could even go sometime this week when you're here. Your dad told me you're staying another couple of weeks."

My family's never really had the money to spend on new paint or fancy linens. The idea of getting new things makes me feel like I'm betraying my own mother, but at the same time, I appreciate how Leah's reaching out and making me feel welcome. I haven't felt totally welcome anywhere in a long time.

"Going shopping would be nice," I say quietly.

Leah takes an extended sip from her coffee mug. We sit in

an awkward silence, playing with our phones, until finally Dad appears. He's wearing a polo shirt tucked into his jeans on what's expected to be a one-hundred-degree day in Chicago. Dad has clearly lost it.

He squeezes Leah's shoulder and sits down next to her.

"Mari," Dad starts. "Leah and I talked last night, and we'd love to have you live here with us next year when you're in college."

"Thank you!" I say. Relief rushes through me like a blast of cool air on a hot day.

Leah pulls a deep breath, glancing from Dad to me. "Mari, I'm sorry. Your dad told me a little bit about how you're feeling. I can't say I know or understand how you feel, but I can listen. I'm sorry for how my actions affected you, I truly am." Leah clasps her hands together and looks down at them.

"Okay," I say quietly. "Thanks."

"I'm sorry too," Dad says. His voice cracks.

I can tell it took a lot for him to say that, but it's not enough. Not really. *Sorry* only goes so far.

"I'm so happy I met your dad," Leah adds. "I never met anyone I wanted to be with before him."

He smiles at her. Again, his ears turn red. It's sweet, but also makes me kind of want to barf. I don't need to hear this much info about my dad's love life.

"Speaking of meeting people," Leah starts, "From what Sierra said, it sounds like T.J.'s a nice guy. I'd like to meet him."

I shrug. "It's not like he's my boyfriend or anything."

"He could be though, right?" Leah says.

Dad grunts unhappily.

"I don't know," I say. "He could be a good friend." I shrug and rub my palms together nervously.

Dad and Leah glance at each other.

"You don't want to date him?" Dad asks.

"I don't want to risk it. Not after seeing how your affair affected Mom. I don't want to be hurt."

This is true, but even as I'm saying the words, T.J.'s smiling face appears in my mind. Based on everything I've learned about him over the past couple of days, I can't see him turning his back on me, on us. Even after I left him standing alone on the boat, he came back to help me.

Leah pats Dad's arm as he leans over and covers his eyes. "I'm truly sorry, Ladybug. Please don't base your life on things that went wrong between your mother and me... If you like this guy, I'm sure I will too."

I clear my throat. "I wouldn't want to fall for someone... and have them leave." I can't imagine the pain of falling in love, only to see him gone. "People in my life have already left. And it sucks. Dad, you left physically, and Mom left me in an entirely different way... She'll never be the mom I want or need."

Dad and Leah are both crying now. He glances at her. "I could've handled things with you and your mother better, Mari. I'm so sorry I left the way I did, and for how things have turned out. I promise I'm going to help you get what you need, and I'll help with your mother too. I'll do what I can to make this right. I want you to feel safe, okay?"

I don't know that I can ever forgive my dad. I won't be able to forget what he did or set it aside.

I look up at his face. It's full of regret. He rubs his eyes.

Our relationship will never be the same, no matter how hard we try to repair it.

But I could try to move forward and make something new.

My mind floats back to what T.J. said last night. How one wrong choice can set you on a path you were never meant to be on. I've let my parents' actions set me on a direction I never meant to go.

Here and now? I want to choose my way.

T.J.

"I can't believe you won backstage passes."

Tyler and I follow the radio station's instructions to pick up backstage bracelets from the WGTP rep. She's wearing a WGTP T-shirt and a lanyard around her neck.

Her face falls. "Oh, we were hoping you'd bring the girl from your posts."

"I'm sorry, she couldn't make it. But I brought my brother."

He sticks out a hand to shake hers. "Hey, I'm Tyler," he says with a suddenly deep movie-announcer voice.

Her eyes light up at him. "I'm Jenna."

I swear. Can he go ten minutes without seducing a woman?

Jenna leads us to a trailer, where we say hello to the band and are quickly ushered to get our picture taken with them. I can't wait to post this on Instagram.

While Tyler is asking the drummer questions, I take a deep breath and approach Adam Tracy. As I stick out my hand, I notice the tattoos racing up and down his arms. "I'm a big fan of your cover art."

His eyes widen. He sweeps his messy brown hair off his forehead. "Nobody ever mentions it. Surprised you know about that."

"I love your covers. What made you decide to do it?"

"Art, you mean?"

"Yeah," I say.

He shrugs. "I need a backup in case music doesn't work out, you know?"

I laugh, loving that art is his backup. Normally it's the other way around: people have a backup in case the art doesn't work out.

Mari was right yesterday. People are always going to want art. The Renaissance happened after the Black Plague. Art grew out of that horrible time and made everyone happy. People go to the movies, stare at art on Instagram and in museums, read books, write poetry.

Art is a constant.

"Art is your backup?" I ask Adam again, just to make sure I heard him correctly.

"It's a solid career, if you go after commercial opportunities in addition to exploring the art you personally love."

"Commercial, like designing the logos and banners for Lollapalooza?"

"Yeah, people are always gonna want graphics and cartoons and animated movies. I don't know how well it all pays, but there's plenty of work for artists."

"Thanks. That's good to know."

Adam crosses his arms, considering me. I check out the tattoos on his knuckles. Some sort of symbols?

"Are you an artist?" he asks.

I nod. "I like painting and graffiti and designs."

"Got anything you can show me?"

I turn on my screen and scroll to my tattoo design.

Adam looks over my shoulder at it. "That's good, man." He studies it more critically. "But have you considered doing it in silver, like the color of chain link? Maybe red for the dragon is too literal?"

"Yeah, maybe." I'm tempted to agree with him because he's Adam Tracy but decide not to. It's my tattoo and it's about what I want, not what anyone else thinks. Not Tyler, not Adam Tracy, not anybody. Me. "I like the red, though."

"Go for it then."

Go for it. That's when I make my decision. When I get home, I'm telling Mom and Dad I don't want to do business. That I have other goals.

And I'm not hesitating any longer: I'm making an appointment to get my tattoo. Maybe I'll keep that a secret, though, so Mom doesn't murder me.

"Tracy," a voice calls out, and Adam looks over his shoulder. "We're about to go on. Gotta go." Adam bumps my fist. "Nice meeting you, man. Stick with the art, okay? Give your info to our manager. I'll reach out."

Holy shit! He wants to be able to contact me! This couldn't have gone better.

As Tyler and I are leaving the trailer, I notice an outdoor lounge area next door. It's fancy, with cushy armchairs, TV screens, and tables full of snacks and drinks. I'm ogling the setup when I'm supposed to be heading back out to watch the concert with the rest of the masses, but then I see her.

Millie Jade.

Mari's favorite singer ever.

Mari's going to be so pissed she wasn't my plus-one. Millie Jade is right over there.

Tyler always says if I want something, I have to ask for it.

He'd say, *Be confident, Teej.*

What do I have to lose? The worst thing that could happen is that a security guard tackles me to the ground and boots me from the premises. A muscular guard pressing my face into hot asphalt would suck royally.

But for Mari? Sure, why not.

After a deep breath, I walk toward Millie Jade.

"T.J.?" Jenna says. "You're supposed to stay with me. I'll get in trouble—"

"Teej?" Tyler calls out, but I don't stop. I have to do this.

Millie's sipping from a mug and scrolling on an iPad. I glance around to see if any guard trolls are about to take me out, but the area is clear.

"Hi." My voice shakes.

Millie Jade raises her chin and looks at me. Her eyebrows furrow.

"My friend is a huge fan of yours," I blurt out. "You're

her favorite singer ever. She came to Lollapalooza just to see you."

The guarded expression turns into a small smile.

An assistant comes out of a trailer and hurries over to Millie. "I'm sorry, Millie, I know you wanted a few minutes to meditate." He points at me. "You. Get gone." The assistant adjusts his headpiece. "I'm calling security."

"Okay, okay, I'm going. Thanks," I say to Millie. "Mari isn't going to believe this."

"Wait." The assistant pauses and takes a harder look at me. "You look familiar... You're the guy from that tweet! The one Chrissy Teigen retweeted."

I nod.

"Oh!" Millie says with a sigh. "That was so cute." She leans to the side and looks around and past me. "Where's your friend? The cute girl in the picture? Is she the one who likes my music?"

"I won a backstage pass to meet the guys from If We Were Giants, and since my brother loves them, Mari suggested that he come backstage with me. She'll be so upset she didn't get to meet you."

The singer sets her iPad down and stands up. "Where'd you say she is?"

"She's coming to your show. She probably already got a good spot out there in the crowd."

His mouth hanging open, Tyler edges closer to us. He's looking back and forth between Millie and me wide-eyed like he's watching a shark ride an elephant or something.

He whispers, "When I said you should talk to lots of different girls to figure out what you want, I didn't mean this."

She holds up a hand and another guy wearing a headset and microphone seemingly appears out of nowhere. "Jamie, can you get me a backstage pass bracelet, please?"

The guy nods, and my heart nearly stops.

"Let's invite her back here."

Mari

On our way into Grant Park with Megan, Sierra loops her arm through my elbow. "I'm so glad you're staying for a couple more weeks!"

"Me too."

"We can go to the beach and ride bikes and see if we can score another invitation to get more of Krysti's strawberry daiquiris and we can hang out with T.J. again—"

"I need more of those daiquiris!" Megan announces.

"He's going home tonight," I say. "He won't be back for college for a few weeks."

"That stinks," Megan says. Sierra keeps taking peeks at her. I don't blame her—Megan looks stunning in a bright pink sleeveless romper and combat boots.

"What happened with you and T.J. last night?" Megan asks.

"Mostly walked around and talked," I say.

"Mostly?" Sierra nudges me. "Did anything else happen?"

"I kissed his cheek. That's it."

Sierra and Megan huff at each other.

"I worry I blew it with him," I say.

Sierra gives me a sly grin. "Does that mean you might be interested?"

"It's easy with him."

Sierra and Megan look at each other, almost as if communicating telepathically. I wouldn't be surprised if they were.

As we continue making our way into the park to find a place to stand for the Millie Jade concert, I replay my day with T.J. in my mind. How he cleaned the bird poop out of my hair while simultaneously laughing his ass off. Him remembering I love Garrett's popcorn. His encouragement to fight for what's best for me.

Being around him is everything, but still very simple. I want to know more about him. Talk to him whenever I want.

Suddenly my phone buzzes with a text. I check the screen to find it's from him. Wow. Did he know I was thinking of him?

T.J.: Come behind the Perry's stage. Trailer #68.

I furrow my eyebrows at my screen. What could this be about? Did Tyler decide to break into a trailer and throw a party?

"I'll be back," I shout to Sierra over the music. I push and shove my way through the crowd in T.J.'s direction. Someone steps on my toe. An elbow catches me in the shoulder. Ouch.

I've had a great time at Lollapalooza, but I'm gonna need another vacation to recover. My bruises have bruises, and based on my sunburn, you'd think I've been sunbathing on Mercury.

When I try to walk behind the stage, scary security guys

block me like a brick wall. One man is so big I wouldn't be surprised if he picked me up above his head to carry me out of here. He could probably beat up the Rock.

I text T.J.: Can't get back there.

The security guys are staring me down, so I step backward, knocking into somebody.

"Watch it!" A woman shoves me to the side, and the hair on the back of my neck stands up.

What if I get stuck in another mosh pit? What if I get knocked to the ground again? I'm about to take off when I hear someone shout my name. "Mari?" A man wearing a lanyard and headset comes over to the fence.

"Yeah! That's me!"

He taps the beefy security guy's shoulder, and I'm granted access. What the hell?

The man snaps a plastic bracelet around my wrist and leads me backstage. My heart races so fast it might explode. What is going on? Did T.J. get permission to bring another person backstage to meet that band?

I follow the man up three wooden stairs into a trailer and look around at the lavish leather furniture that's far nicer than my living room back home.

T.J. struts forward. He takes my hands in his, cradling them like I'm a treasure.

I blurt out, "I had a great day with you yesterday. It was the best day of my life."

He pauses. Blinks. "Me too."

I want a chance. He's worth it. *I'm worth it.* "I know you're going home tonight, but I have to tell you..."

"Tell me what?"

I swallow, and make another choice. A choice for me. "I like you."

He slowly smiles. "I like you too."

"Can I keep texting you? Like, after today?"

He stares into my eyes. "What are you saying?"

"Right now we live really far apart, and I'm not sure if I'll get to move here soon or if I'll only be able to visit more often, but I want to see you again."

He carefully wraps a hand around the back of my neck and leans forward to peck my lips. "I want to see you too."

I tiptoe my fingers up his spine and grip his T-shirt in my fist. "Can you be patient with me? I've never done this before, and I don't know how—"

"I've never done this either. We'll figure it out together."

My eyes are watering. "I talked to my dad. I'm sticking around here for another couple of weeks. He's going to talk to a lawyer and see if he might be able to get custody of me."

T.J. pulls me into a deep hug. "I'm so glad you talked to him. Are you happy?"

"I have no idea what's going to happen next, but I feel so much better." I press my cheek against T.J.'s chest. For the first time in a long time, everything feels okay. "T.J.? Why are you in this trailer? Where's your band?" I glance about, pushing my glasses back up on my nose. "The Giant people?"

He shakes his head with an amused smile. "If We Were Giants."

Someone emerges from another room. But it's not a man. It's a woman with pink hair wearing a white minidress. Millie Jade!

"Oh my God!" I exclaim. "You're my favorite."

"Thanks, girl."

She gives me a light hug, and I feel like I might faint. "You're the sweetest," she says.

A photographer snaps pictures of her with me, and then another with T.J. and Tyler too. A woman wearing a WGTP T-shirt is grinning broadly like she hit the lottery.

After thanking Millie profusely, T.J. and I walk back out into the crowd, hand in hand.

"I left Sierra over there." I point toward the area near the stage where Millie is set to perform in a few minutes. The band opening for her is still going strong. I spot Sierra and Megan dancing wildly together, holding hands. Sierra lifts her arms up making a bridge for Megan to twirl under in a circle. They laugh and smile at each other.

As we walk up, T.J. wraps an arm around my waist and pulls me close. He kisses the side of my head. Something tells me we'll have a hard time keeping our hands off each other today.

"Oh my God," Sierra squeals as we approach her. "You guys are together?"

"We're getting to know each other," T.J. responds tactfully, and it's the perfect thing to say.

Sierra moves next to me and speaks through her clenched teeth. "Did you change your mind?"

"Yeah, I guess I finally woke up and realized the chance to be close with him outweighs my fears, you know?"

At my words, Sierra stands up straight. She pulls her long blond braid over her shoulder and plays with it as she turns to look at Megan.

Megan and T.J. are now dancing together along to the band.

Sierra suddenly beelines toward Megan, taking her by the elbow. Megan turns toward Sierra, tilting her head back to look up at her. Megan's mouth falls open at the look of care on Sierra's face. Sierra pushes Megan's braids behind one of her ears, leans in, and kisses her.

Kisses her!

My heart stops for a moment because Megan's eyes are wide open like she's been shocked with electricity—and I'm worried about how she'll react, but then she closes her eyes and leans into the kiss, bracing her hands on Sierra's shoulders. I'm surprised they're able to kiss because they're both smiling so damn hard.

T.J. and I yell "Woo!" and cheer for them along with a bunch of strangers in the crowd.

Tyler arrives holding a beer. "What'd I miss?"

T.J. gestures at Tyler's plastic cup. "Dude, it's not even noon."

"Well, it's five o'clock somewhere, and I needed it. I asked Millie if she'd want to hang out sometime."

"And?" I say.

Tyler takes a long gulp. "It was a hard pass."

"But at least you had the courage to try," T.J. says, which makes Tyler laugh and raise his plastic cup in a toast.

When Millie takes the stage, I scream my lungs out for her. Sierra, Megan, and I jump up and down and cheer, beginning to sing along with her.

Millie's still my favorite singer, but after this weekend, I'm not sure how much I buy into her song "Destiny."

If I'd stuck with the idea that your destiny is your destiny and it keeps coming around to find you, no matter what, then this weekend never would've happened.

I made the choice to visit Chicago. If I hadn't, I never would've met T.J.

I'm making my own choices from now on.

I reach out a hand to him and he pulls me close against his chest. His blue eyes are endless.

"Hi," he says.

"Hi."

With a smile, I get up on tiptoes as he dips his head to kiss me.

The crowd roars as the song ends, but all I can hear are our two hearts beating as one.

EPILOGUE

ONE YEAR LATER

Dad and I walk our usual route to the beach.

We descend down the steps into the tunnel under Lake Shore Drive. As always, I hold my breath to avoid the stench and try not to step in any puddles. Especially the one full of questionable green goo.

Ever since I moved to Chicago to live with Dad full-time last October, we take a walk together every Saturday morning. It's our thing. It did get a little dicey once winter came and we saw several blizzards in a row, but we've made it a point to get outside and spend time together.

I'm tiptoeing around a puddle, passing the painting of Obama in a Cubs cap, when a patch of sunlight catches my eye. Hey, that mural wasn't here last week.

I stop in front of it. Before T.J., I never paid much attention to graffiti. Now I look at it all the time. I see it for what it is: art.

The new mural comes into focus. Brown curly hair. Glasses. A girl leaning on her chin on a fist. A brown bracelet ringing her wrist. Tulips of every color—*even pastels*—surround her.

"Wow," Dad says. "This one's good. I haven't seen it before... It looks like you, Ladybug."

"Dad, I think it is me."

Sierra and I stand outside our apartment building, waiting for our Ryde.

A silver Lexus rolls up. Now this is what I'm talking about.

I open the door to the back seat, slide in, and find T.J.

His fingers slide effortlessly between mine. His other hand plays with the leather bracelet around my wrist, the one he gave me. As always, it's hard for us to keep our hands to ourselves.

"Ready?" he asks.

"Can't wait."

"Wait, where's Megan?" Tyler asks.

"Meeting us there," Sierra says with a little smile on her face.

The car pulls away from the curb and heads downtown. I lean my head on T.J.'s shoulder as he caresses my hand. His fingers tiptoe down to my thigh and gently caress it.

This summer apart has been rough for us. After being together most of the school year, he went home to Madison to live with his parents for the summer, and I visited my mom for a few weeks. It went okay. I don't know if we'll ever have the loving relationship I'd like to have with my mom, but she didn't yell or hurt me in any way. My aunt stayed with us when I visited, and Mom's continuing to go to therapy, as agreed upon with the judge and social worker.

Just like the past few summers, Austin and I spent a lot of nights sitting in the back of his pickup truck and talking, looking up at the stars. You can see them much more clearly in Tennessee than in Chicago. We also went to Bonnaroo together in Manchester. He was very impressed with my new tip to wear heavy boots instead of our usual sneakers and flip-flops.

He's been dating this sweet girl Lydia who's always onboard to ride four-wheelers and Jet-Ski on Lake Normandy with him, and he seems very happy, but he's worried because they're going to different colleges an hour apart—her in Georgia and him in Tennessee.

Now, T.J. and I are both back in Chicago, and I'm beyond happy. No more video chats every night; instead, I can see him in person. T.J.'s starting sophomore year, and since I'll be a freshman, we'll get to see each other every day. Now that I'll be starting college, maybe I can even spend the night at his place.

I allow myself a naughty little daydream, in which I pull him into his dorm room between classes and yank off his shirt. Though, my daydreams are never as good as the real thing. Our chemistry is seismic.

I haven't told him I love him, but I do. I'm totally in love.

I check him out, dragging a fingertip along his tanned forearm. His muscles are stronger than ever. Spray paint dots his hands.

I run my fingers over the paint and raise a playful eyebrow. "What have you been up to?"

"It's a surprise."

"You know I hate surprises."

"You'll love this one," Tyler says from the front seat. "C'mon, Teej. Show her now."

T.J. swipes on his phone and scrolls. He passes his phone over to me. It's a photo of my mural in the Lake Shore Drive tunnel. A new picture is next to it.

T.J. painted himself looking at an orange sun shaped like a heart.

T.J.

As we're driving downtown to Lollapalooza, I can't wait to get her alone later tonight.

My blood is on fire.

Her fingers trace the specks of dried paint splattered across the backs of my hands.

I can't wait to show her my new mural in person. *Tomorrow*, I decide. I'll take her tomorrow.

You can't see it in the picture I took, but I wrote her a note in bright white paint.

I love you, Mari

And based on how she's staring at me now, I know she'll say it back.

Acknowledgments

I can be a shy person, and it takes me a while to warm up to new people. It's not something I talk about much because I've always been careful about sharing my emotions and feelings with others—even those I consider to be close friends. My family had a bad falling out when I was a teenager and it changed who I was as a person. It made me scared of letting new people into my life. In writing *The Pick-Up*, I've tried to share a little bit about how I felt and show that no matter what has happened to you in the past, you can always choose to make changes and go down a new path that's right for you. Be willing to take the risk of accepting new people in—you might meet some of your best friends that way. Don't let fear make choices for you. Live the life you want to lead.

I had a wonderful time working on this book with my editor, Molly Cusick, and I hope to get the chance to work with her again in the future. Thank you to Wendy McClure, Cassie Gutman, and everyone at Sourcebooks for helping me to push this story over the finish line and out into the world. As always, thanks to my wonderful agent, Jim McCarthy, for his endless enthusiasm and support. Thank you to Andrea Soule and Gail Yates for originally brainstorming this book with me and for always being there.

I've had the opportunity to spend a lot of time in Chicago for my job. It's one of my favorite cities. Thank you to everyone there, including folks who work for the Convention Center and the City of Chicago, who have been so kind to me and taught me about the city. I had planned to attend Lollapalooza in 2020 so I could gather final details for this story, but was unable to visit due to COVID-19. Luckily author Lisa Maxwell attended in the past and told me lots of great details. Thank you to author Tiffany Schmidt for helping me figure out character motivations—you're always so good at that!

And finally, thank you to my readers! Keep working hard, stay open-minded, and go after your dreams.

Don't miss another rom-com from Miranda Kenneally

LOVE IS THE TOUGHEST GAME TO PLAY.

TURN THE PAGE FOR A PREVIEW!

A HAIL MARY AND A HAREM

I once read that football was invented so people wouldn't notice summer ending. But I couldn't wait for summer vacation to end. I couldn't wait for football. Football, dominator of fall—football, love of my life.

"Blue forty-two! Blue forty-two! Red seventeen!" I yell.

The cue is red seventeen. JJ hikes me the ball. The defense is blitzing. JJ slams into a freshman safety, knocking him to the ground. The rest of my offensive line destroys the defense. Nice. The field's wide open, but my wide receiver isn't where he's supposed to be.

"What the hell, Higgins?" I mutter to myself.

Dancing on my tiptoes, I scan the end zone and find Sam Henry instead and hurl the ball. It flies through the air, a perfect spiral, heading right where I wanted it to go. He catches the ball, spikes it, and does this really stupid dance. Henry looks like a freaking ballerina. With his thin frame and girly blond hair, he actually could be the star of the New York Ballet.

I'm gonna give him hell for his dance.

This is my senior year at Hundred Oaks High, and I'm captain, so I'm allowed to keep my players in line. Even though he's my best friend, Henry has always been a showoff. His antics get us penalties.

Through the speaker in my helmet, I hear Coach Miller say, "Nice throw. This is your year, Woods. You're going to lead us to the state championship. I can feel it... Hit the showers." What the coach actually means? *I know you're not going to blow it in the final seconds of the championship game like you did last year.*

And he's right. I can't.

The University of Alabama called last week—on the first day of school—to tell me a recruiter is coming to watch me play on Friday night. And then a very fancy-looking letter arrived, inviting me to visit campus in September. An official visit. If they like what they see, they'll sign me in February.

I can't screw this season up.

I pull my helmet off and grab a bottle of Gatorade and my playbook. Most of the guys are already goofing off and heading over to watch cheerleading practice across the field, but I ignore them and look up into the stands.

I spot Mom sitting with Carter's dad, a former NFL player. My dad isn't here, of course. Asshole.

Lots of parents come to watch our practices because football is the big thing to do around here. Here being Franklin,

Tennessee, home of the Hundred Oaks Red Raiders, eight-time state champions.

Mom always comes to practice—she's been supporting me ever since Pop Warner youth football days, but sometimes she worries I'll get hurt, even though the worst thing that's ever happened was a concussion. Sophomore year, when JJ took a breather, the coach brought in this idiot to play center, the idiot didn't cover me, and I got slammed hard.

Otherwise, I'm a rock. No knee problems, no broken limbs.

Dad never comes to my practices and rarely comes to games. People think it's because he's busy, because he's Donovan Woods, the starting quarterback for the Tennessee Titans. But the truth is he doesn't want me playing football. Why wouldn't a famous quarterback want his kid to follow in the family footsteps? Well, he does. He loves that my brother, Mike, a junior in college, plays for the University of Tennessee and led his team to a win at the Sugar Bowl last year. So what the hell is Dad's problem with my playing ball?

I'm a girl.

After chugging a bunch of Gatorade, I go find Higgins, who's already attempting to flirt with Kristen Markum, the most idiotic of cheerleaders. I take Higgins aside, avoiding her Darth Vader stare, and say, "Next time try finishing your route instead of staring at Kristen, will you?"

His face goes all red before he nods. "Okay."

"Great."

Then I go pull a sophomore cornerback aside to speak

privately. Duckett's a couple inches shorter than me, so I put a hand on his shoulder and walk him down the sideline.

"On that last play, where I threw the long pass to Henry, you left him wide open. And I know how fast he is, but you can't let that happen in the game. You were totally out of position."

Duckett drops his head and nods at me. "Got it, Woods."

I pat his back with my playbook as I take another sip of Gatorade and wipe the dribble from my mouth. "Good. We're counting on you Friday night. I'm sure Coach is going to start you."

Duckett smiles as he puts his helmet under an arm and heads toward the locker room.

"Awesome job today, guys," I say to a couple of my offensive linemen, then jog over to Henry and look up at him.

He says, "What's good, Woods?"

"Nice move faking out Duckett on that last play."

Henry laughs. "I know, right?"

"Would you quit it with the dancing?"

He grins at me, his green eyes lighting up as he drags a hand through his blond curls. "You know you love it."

Smiling, I shove his chest. "Whatever."

He shoves me back. "Want to come out to eat with us?"

"Who's us?"

"Me and JJ..."

"And?"

"Oh, let's see...Samantha and Marie and Lacey and Kristen."

I stick my tongue out before saying, "Shit, no."

"We're going to Pete's Roadhouse," he says, wiggling his eyebrows.

Damn it. I love going there. It's one of those restaurants where they let you throw peanut shells all over the floor. Still, I reply, "Can't. My brother said he'd watch film with me tonight."

Henry gets this hurt look on his face. "Come on, Woods. You know I want to go to Michigan more than anything, and I'm working hard, but you've been holed up every night since you heard that Alabama is coming to opening game."

I suck in a breath. "Right—I've only got three days left to get perfect."

"You're already, like, one hundred times the quarterback your brother was in high school, you know."

I grin at Henry. "Thanks," I say, even though it's not true.

He wipes sweat off his forehead with his red and black jersey. "How about I come over and watch film with you instead?"

"What about Samantha and Marie and Lacey and Kristen?"

He glances over at the cheerleaders. "They'd wait a year for me."

I shove him again, and he laughs. "Nah, it's okay," I say. "I'm glad you're going out with girls again, even if Kristen is Satan's sister."

"I'd never fool around with Kristen—I have standards, you know."

"Bullshit," I say as JJ and Carter walk up.

With his helmet in hand, JJ drapes an arm around Henry's shoulders. I'm surprised Henry's skinny knees don't buckle under JJ's 275 pounds. "You in trouble again, man?" JJ asks in his deep voice.

"Woods doesn't appreciate my dancing skills."

"No one likes your *dancing skills*," JJ replies. He nods at me. "You in for the Roadhouse, Woods?"

"Can't. Gotta study," I say, holding up the playbook.

"Take a break," JJ says.

"I bet you'd go if they'd picked a place that makes real food, like Michel's Bistro or Julien L'Auberge in Nashville," Carter says in a ridiculous French accent, and JJ, Henry, and I burst out laughing at him.

"Hell no," I say. "All I need is a big slab of meat and a bunch of peanut shells to throw all over the floor."

"Blasphemy," Carter replies.

"You're not going either?" I ask Carter.

He focuses on his cleats before saying, "Can't—it's a practice night, remember?" He's, like, the only person I know whose parents never say anything about school nights—it's always about football practice and games in the Carter household.

"Come on, Woods," Henry whines. "Just for an hour or two."

I hate saying no to him. "If I get through four hours of Alabama film tonight, I'll come out tomorrow."

"Fine," Henry says, smiling.

"As long as you don't bring your harem." I jerk my head at the group of cheerleaders hovering ten yards away near a goal post, making googly eyes at the guys.

"But we're a package deal," he says with a laugh.

"That's 'cause all you ever think about is your package," JJ replies.

"And you don't?" I snap and JJ punches my shoulder, causing me to stumble backward. We all crack up again.

And then two cheerleaders come up and start fawning over Henry and JJ. What took them so long?

JJ and Lacey start kissing as if winning the state championship depends on it, and Samantha intertwines her fingers with Henry's and smiles up at him. Then Kristen and Marie come over, because cheerleaders travel in packs.

"Nice practice today, Jordan," Marie says, giving me a smile. "That quarterback sneak of yours is great."

"Did Henry tell you to say that?" I ask, staring down at her.

"No," she mutters, looking at her pompoms as she ruffles them.

JJ and Lacey break apart, much like unsnapping Velcro, as Kristen says, "Don't get Jordan started, Marie. We'll be here all night listening to stats and pointers on pitching footballs..."

"They're called *passes*, Kristen," I reply. "Don't think too hard. I hear it makes your hair frizzy."

"Ha, ha," Kristen replies, but she subconsciously smooths her brown hair with a hand. It takes everything I've got not to burst out laughing when I see Samantha and Lacey patting their hair too. I sneak a peek at Henry, JJ, and Carter, and they start snickering again. So does Marie.

"Call if you change your mind about getting food," Henry says to me and Carter, and we all knock fists before Henry and JJ trudge off with their fan club toward the locker rooms.

I clutch my playbook to my chest and for a moment, I feel a pang of loneliness and wish that I had asked Henry to come over. He's been sad since his girlfriend dumped him a couple months ago, so he'd probably appreciate the company. Especially since he's been spending time with girls who think a Hail Mary is a prayer to Jesus's mom.

But he'd just distract me—and I need to concentrate on performing well for Alabama.

"Carter, let's go home," I hear his dad call out from the first row of the metal bleachers. "Your mom's keeping dinner warm until we're done working out."

"Have fun watching film," Carter says. "I'll be wishing I'm you as I do sit-ups with Dad tonight."

Carter jogs over to his dad, who immediately starts talking and gesturing with his hands, probably giving a play-by-play critique of how practice went.

I wish Dad would talk with me like that.

————————

Back at home, I take a seat at the kitchen table and open my playbook. I peel a banana as I study the formation for Red Rabbit, this super cool flea-flicker play Coach wants us to try tomorrow. It'll be hard, but Henry and I can pull it off.

Mom comes in, lays her pruning shears and gardening gloves

on the counter, and then pours a glass of water. "Why didn't you go out with your friends tonight?"

"I'm not ready for opening game," I reply, training my eyes on the *X*s and *O*s scrawled across the paper.

"From what I've seen at practice, you're definitely ready. I don't want you to burn out."

"Never."

"Maybe you need a massage. A spa day...so you'll be all fresh and relaxed for Friday. We could go on Thursday after I'm done volunteering at the hospital."

I slowly lift my head to stare at Mom. *Yeah, I'm sure the guys would take me seriously if I show up with pink fingernails on Friday night.* "No, but thanks." I give her a smile so I won't hurt her feelings.

She smiles back. "What are you planning to wear on your trip to Alabama?"

I shrug. "I dunno. Cleats? And my Hundred Oaks sweats?"

Mom sips her water. "I was thinking maybe we could go shopping for a dress."

"Nah, but thanks."

God, if I wore a dress, the Alabama guys would laugh me right out of Tuscaloosa, right back to some pitiful Division II school. "The Alabama head coach is a big Baltimore fan. Maybe I'll wear a Ravens jersey."

Mom laughs. "Dad would kick you out of the house."

"Why am I kicking my daughter out of the house?" the *great* Donovan Woods asks as he comes into the kitchen and gives Mom a kiss and a hug.

"No reason," I mutter and flip a page in my playbook.

Dad grabs a bottle of Gatorade, the strawberry-plum shit he does advertising for, and takes a gulp. He's still buff as ever, but his black hair has started to turn salt-and-peppery. At forty-three years old, Dad has tried to retire after each of the five previous seasons, but he always comes back for some reason or another. Over the years, this has become a joke to sportscasters, so unless we want to get yelled at, we never ask when he's actually going to retire.

He stares down at my playbook and shakes his head.

"You coming to my game on Friday?" I ask Dad.

He looks at Mom when he replies, "Maybe. I'll think about it."

"Okay..."

"How about I take you and Henry fishing on Saturday morning before we go to your brother's game?" Dad smiles at me expectantly.

What total bullshit. He'll go to Mike's game, but won't come to mine? And he tries to suck up by asking me to go fishing?

"No thanks," I say.

The grin dissolves from Dad's face. "Maybe next weekend then," he says softly.

"And maybe you could come to my game on Friday," I mumble to myself. "Mom, where's Mike?" I'm anxious to start watching more Alabama film. Even though I've watched hundreds of college and pro games, I love getting an expert opinion and, well, Dad's never willing to give it.

"Oh," Mom replies. "His coach called a team meeting. Mike said to tell you he's sorry."

"That's cool," I say quietly.

Mom starts telling Dad all about her roses and sunflowers, gesturing out the kitchen window toward the garden. "The sunflowers have almost reached a state of Zen, don't you think?"

Dad wraps his arms around Mom, and I swear I hear him murmur, "I'm in a state of Zen right now too."

Before I reach a state of upchuck, I grab my playbook and a package of chocolate-chip cookies and head downstairs to our basement, where I turn on the TV and put in a DVD of last year's national championship game—Alabama vs. Texas.

I flip off the lights, settle down on one of the leather sofas, and dig into the cookies as I push the play button on the remote.

So. My friends are off hooking up with cheerleaders.

My dad cares more about sunflowers reaching a state of Zen than my feelings.

At least I've got football.

It's been my life since I was seven, but sometimes Henry says I need to spend less time focusing and start "living life like I'm going to hell tomorrow."

But I feel like a normal teenager. Well, as normal as I can be. I mean, obviously I think Shawn Mendes is a mega-hunk, but I'm also more than six feet tall and can launch a football fifty yards.

Other ways I'm not normal?

A girl who hangs with an entire football team must hook up all the time, right?

Nope.

I've never had a boyfriend. Hell, I've never even kissed a guy. The closest I've ever come to a kiss happened just this past summer, but it was a joke. At a party, one of those cheerleaders suggested we all play a game of seven minutes in heaven, you know, the game where you go into a closet and kiss? Somehow Henry and I got sent into the closet together, and of course we didn't kiss, but we ended up in a mad thumb-wrestling match. Which turned into a shoving match. Which turned into everyone thinking we'd hooked up in the closet. Yeah, right. He's like my brother.

It's not that guys aren't interested in me, because they are, it's that most of the guys I know are either:

    a.   Shorter than me

    b.   Pansies

    c.   On my team

    d.   All of the above

I would never let myself date guys on my team. And I'm not interested in any of them anyway. Riding buses to and from games for years has turned me off to all of them 'cause one bus ride with my team produces more gas than a landfill.

Besides, I don't have time for guys, and if I suddenly were to start acting like a girl, the team might not take me seriously. And I can't afford to lose my confidence—because I'm the star of the Hundred Oaks Red Raiders.

The star Alabama will love on Friday night.

About the Author

Miranda Kenneally grew up in Manchester, Tennessee, a quaint little town where nothing cool ever happened until after she left. Now, Manchester is the home of Bonnaroo. Growing up, Miranda wanted to become an author, a major-league baseball player, a country music singer, or an interpreter for the United Nations. Instead, she became an author who also works for the U.S. Department of State in Washington, DC. She enjoys reading and writing young adult literature and loves *Star Trek*, music, sports, Mexican food, going to the gym, Twitter, and coffee. She lives in Northern Virginia, with her husband, Don, and cats, Brady and Ryan, and dog, Jack. Visit mirandakenneally.com.

FIREreads

#getbooklit

Your hub for the hottest young adult books!

Visit us online and sign up for our
newsletter at FIREreads.com

 @sourcebooksfire

 sourcebooksfire

 firereads.tumblr.com